WHO'S NEW AT THE ZOO

Janette
Oke

Other Janette Oke
Children's Books in this Series:

SPUNKY'S DIARY
NEW KID IN TOWN
THE PRODIGAL CAT
DUCKTAILS
THE IMPATIENT TURTLE
A COTE OF MANY COLORS
PRAIRIE DOG TOWN
MAURY HAD A LITTLE LAMB
TROUBLE IN A FUR COAT
THIS LITTLE PIG
PORDY'S PRICKLY PROBLEM

Copyright © 1994
Bethel Publishing Company
All Rights Reserved

Published by
Bethel Publishing Company
1819 South Main Street
Elkhart, Indiana 46516

Cover Illustration by
Brenda Mann

Printed in the United States of America

ISBN 0-934998-55-8

Dedicated
to one I have not yet met
but already love
and can't wait to welcome,
Katie's and Kristie's
new baby sister
or brother.

A special Thank You
to Rob Sutherland,
Keeper of the Gorillas
at the
Calgary Zoo

Table of Contents

Chapter One

Introductions

I wasn't ready to wake up yet. In my drowsy state I even thought of protesting. It seemed that I had just gotten nicely to sleep. I could have tightened my finger and toe hold on my mother's fur and kept right on dozing but she was moving and my curiosity wouldn't allow me to sleep on. I had to know where we were going.

Slowly I opened my eyes. I always dreaded the first glimpse of light after being bundled up snugly in the comfortable darkness of dreamland. Automatically my hands tightened their grip on Mother's thick, soft fur. I opened one eye enough to let in a little light but it wasn't enough to inform me of our destination. Opening both eyes, I lifted my head to look around.

"Where we goin'?" I mumbled into Mother's fur.

Her free hand reached down and tucked me in close against her but she didn't answer my question.

I pushed back against the hand, trying to position myself for a better look around. Other family members were stirring too.

"What's happenin'?" I asked Mother.

She looked down at me then and gently patted my shoulder.

"The doors will open soon," she answered.

The doors would open. Already I understood about the doors. When the doors opened there would be even more light. And movement and commotion. And noise. Lots of noise. When the doors opened, our rather quiet neighborhood became a totally different place. I don't know where all of the strange creatures came from. But I already knew that Mother, who often seemed to totally ignore them, wasn't fond of all of the company.

I rather looked forward to it. Some of the visitors I had viewed in my brief time of existence were most interesting to watch. They did the most extraordinary things and made the strangest sounds. One was never quite sure what might happen next.

I pushed farther back from Mother. I wished that she wouldn't take me so far away from the big glass window that separated the noisy visitors from our confined space.

"I want to see," I protested.

Mother didn't comment but silently pushed my face up against her furred body. It made me feel like sneezing. I pushed back again.

"I want to see," I said again.

Mother did not respond to my continued protest. However, she did stop moving. We were back from the glass, tucked into a rather dark corner. I couldn't see well at all from there. For a moment, I felt disappointment. Mother settled herself against the concrete wall and shifted me in her arms. I still had handfuls of fur clutched tightly in my fists, but Mother moved me enough to look down into my eyes. I guess I still looked sleepy for she spoke softly, "Sh-h. Go back to sleep now."

She tucked me in closer to her broad chest and stroked my back with one large hand.

I wanted to protest again. I wanted to stay awake to see what would happen when the doors opened. But I was still so sleepy. I was a little hungry, too. I decided to have a light snack and then doze for just a few more minutes. I cuddled up closely to Mother and began to nurse. She pushed back even further into the shadows and held me firmly, securely, in her arms. I forgot all about the doors that were about to open. I didn't care any more. I felt so loved, so content, so cared for. I curled my fingers into Mother's dark fur and let my eyelids shut out the world around me. I'd watch the doors open another day.

* * * * *

When I awoke, the noise was horrendous. It seemed to make Mother a little nervous. I couldn't understand why. The rest of the family didn't seem to mind. In fact, for the most part, they seemed to be oblivious to it. I pushed back from Mother and sat blinking against the brightness, trying to focus my eyes properly so I could get a good look at what was going on.

To my right sat Father. He had his back to the glass lined with all of the stirring, noisy visitors. I wondered if he even knew that they were there. He was picking through a dish, idly turning over and fingering pieces of food. I wondered if he was hungry or just curious as to what was there. He selected something from the lot and lifted it to his nose. He didn't seem to like it for he let it fall from his fingers without taking a bite. Reaching for another bit of the food, he stared at it for a moment and then took a tentative bite. He didn't look too impressed with it either for he spit out what he had taken and dropped the remainder on the concrete floor. Then he reached down to sort through the dish again.

I knew that his preference was oranges. Mother had told me. She wanted to be sure that I never got into trouble by reaching for an orange portion that my father was reaching for. By watching Mother and the other family members, I had learned that my father was the head of the family. It was easy to see that everyone, male or female, young or old, regarded my father as the one in charge. In the family, Father was known as Big Sam but to the strange human "keepers" who visited us daily to bring our food, he was referred to as The Silver Back. Mother said that meant that my father was King. I guess that sort of made me a Prince. I liked that idea.

There were seven of us in the family troop. I was the youngest member. Mother was the dominant female. Being dominant meant that Mother held the highest position of the ladies in our group. She could even tell Nick, the other male in our family, what he could or couldn't do. It made me feel proud when other family members showed Mother the honor and

respect that she deserved.

There were three other females. Mitsy was a friendly, likeable sort. She seemed immensely interested in me and Mother let her help with my care in a guarded sort of way. I liked Mitsy.

Then there was Petunia. I didn't care much for her. She was always agitated about something. The food wasn't good, her bed-nest was too hard, the visitors made too much noise, the sun was too bright, and on and on it went. Even my father slyly turned his back when he saw her approaching.

The other member of the family was Ms. Evangeline. She was very old and usually sat quietly in her favorite corner observing the world through watery eyes. I had the feeling that she didn't approve of all that she saw, but she was not condemning. Occasionally she would shake her head and sigh deeply, but she made no comment. She brushed a shaky hand over her rheumy eyes and blinked at the strangeness of the world around her.

Mother and I often visited old Ms. Evangeline for she didn't stir about much and kept to her own corner nest. She liked to hold me and would gently run her hand over my head or pat me on the shoulder. She didn't say much but she and Mother seemed to communicate without words.

And that was our family.

Oh, I forgot to tell you about Nick. Nick was the only other male in the group. He was much younger and much smaller than my father. Petunia fussed about him constantly declaring him to be young and rude and totally disrespectful. Mother said that he was just impetuous and fun-loving. She stated that he would out-grow his childish pranks. He would soon learn that life was not all fun and games. Gradually, I gathered that there was some strange bond between my mother and young Nick. I didn't understand it but I decided that it didn't matter enough to try to figure it out. Mother kept a close eye on young Nick, yet chose to ignore some of his escapades. However, Petunia ranted and raged and tattled to my father.

"It's your responsibility," she would say. "Your responsibility."

I didn't know what responsibility was and wasn't too sure that my father understood it either, for he never seemed to pay much attention to the angry tirade. He just blinked his eyes, turned his back and continued to feast on the orange sections or scratch his tummy.

I liked my family and I soon learned that we were important to one another. Even though we didn't always see things in the same way, we did care for one another. I believe that any one of the family would have defended another, had the need ever arose. Even Petunia. It was hard for me to imagine her coming to anyone's rescue. Still, in her own way, perhaps she wasn't so bad. Just touchy and cranky. I decided early in life that I would stay out of Petunia's way.

* * * * *

For the first several weeks of my life, I did nothing much more than eat and sleep. I knew that I was growing for I seemed to fit Mother's arms differently. I stayed very close to her. My fingers and toes were always wound tightly in her fur. It gave me a wonderful feeling of security.

I was conscious of our family members as they moved about us and shared in my care as far as Mother would permit. I heard the chatter, the discussions, the debates. From the talk around me I learned about my family and my world. But my life was limited by my close surroundings and my protective mother. I liked it that way. At first. But as I grew, I found that my curiosity grew as well. Surely there was more to life than our concrete home. There had to be interesting things beyond our walls.

The opening of the doors each morning seemed to reaffirm my thinking. I longed to stay awake long enough to discover everything that I could about the exciting world that I had entered. I wished that I didn't fall asleep so easily. I wished that Mother would move closer to the glassed front of our home. I wished that I was more like Nick—up and about on my own. Each time that I started to stir restlessly, Mother just tucked me in more securely. It seemed that she wasn't at all anxious for me to grow up.

Chapter Two

Beyond

One day I realized that we did not live alone. That is, we did live alone in our own home but we were not alone in our concrete world. I was thrilled to learn that we had many neighbors and at once began asking Mother questions.

"Who are *they*?" I began, my voice shaking with excitement. I was looking out beyond our glass wall at a cage next to ours where strange creatures swung back and forth through make-believe branches.

Mother did not even lift her eyes to look in their direction. "Howlers," she answered and continued to nibble on the piece of fruit in her hand.

"What are they doing?" I asked, my eyes wide with wonder.

"Swinging," said Mother.

I sat and watched them. I was amazed at the way they moved through the air.

"Swingin'," I repeated softly, wanting to remember the word. Then I reached out and tugged at Mother's fur. "Why do they do that?" I asked her.

She shook her head. Her eyes still did not lift to the howlers. "It's their way," she said as though that would satisfy me.

But it didn't. Not at all. I watched the neighbors as they swung and leaped and chased one another through the artificial branches and off the sides and even the ceiling of the cage. They seemed to be made of springs—all wound for movement and continually in motion.

"How do they do it?" I asked Mother in awe.

She shrugged as though it was really of no consequence and reached for another piece of sweet potato. Father had already eaten all of the oranges.

I continued to watch. I couldn't believe my eyes. Never had I dreamed that any creature could move as rapidly or as agilely as the howlers were doing. They were strange creatures indeed.

I turned to Mother again and jerked on her coat. "What are they?" I asked her, not quite sure how to word my question.

"Howlers," she answered again, patient with my forgetfulness.

"No," I responded quickly. "No, I don't mean that. What . . . what . . . kind of . . . of animals are they?"

"Howlers," she said again, peeling back a banana so that she could get at the fruit.

"That's their name," I protested, "but what kind of . . . of creatures are they?"

She looked at me and blinked. But she did seem to understand my question. "Family," she said simply.

"Family?"

I was astonished at the answer. I looked at myself, then at Mother and then turned again to the

howlers next door. We weren't anything alike as far
as I could see.

"Family," she said again as though that settled
it.

"But . . . but they aren't anything like . . . like
us," I argued.

Mother nodded her head in agreement with my
observation. "Family, nonetheless," she stated. "Family members don't have to all be alike, you know."

She took another bite of the banana.

"But . . ." I began again.

"They are distant relatives," Mother continued and
seemed to think that was sufficient explanation as
to why we were so different. She moved to reach
for a piece of grapefruit.

"But . . ." I was still sputtering. "Are you sure?"

She looked at me and blinked her eyes twice but
the expression on her face did not change. Peeling
back the rind with her teeth to get at the sweetness
of the fruit, she took a bite. The juice dripped from
her chin but she paid no attention to it. I thought
that she had forgotten my question and was about
to ask it again when she spoke softly. "We are all
family in here. This is the Primate House. We are
different—it's true. Just look around. On this side—
the howlers." She nodded her head toward the cage
where the acrobats were still tirelessly performing.
"And over there," she said, nodding her head in the
other direction, "the chimps. Across the way are the
gibbons and to their left, the orangutans and to their
right, the baboons. And on and on in every direction are more and more family members. You can't

see them all from here. They are all different, but all primates. We are all family."

I felt excitement fill me until I thought that I would explode. We were all family. In some strange way I belonged to all of these exciting creatures in the cages about me. I repeated it to myself—*we were family*. I could hardly wait to get acquainted with every one of them. I felt cheated that I had been shut away from them until now and I wanted to remedy the situation as quickly as possible.

I reached out to give Mother a tug but she paid little attention to me. I was annoyed that she was still intent on eating.

"Hurry," I said.

She blinked again and looked puzzled. She seemed to feel that there was no need to hurry for anything.

"Hurry," I said again.

"Hurry?" she questioned. "Why?"

"I want to go see them," I said excitedly.

Mother reached for a piece of apple. "See who?" she asked without much interest.

"The howlers. The family," I said, tugging at her coat.

Mother blinked again. "See them?" she asked and this time she showed a bit more interest. "What do you mean, see them? You can see them from here."

"No, not see them through the glass—or bars—*see* them. In person. Visit them."

Mother's hand stopped on the way to her mouth. The apple seemed to be forgotten. My demand had captured her full attention.

"You can't do that," she said with emphasis.

Now it was my turn to blink. What did she mean? They were right there—just beyond our home. Not more than a stone's throw away. Why couldn't we go and visit them?

"Why?" I asked dumbly. "Why?"

Mother shifted her weight in an agitated fashion. She didn't seem to know the answer. "Because," she said at last and continued to eat the apple.

"But why?" I insisted.

"It's—it's just not done," she answered and shifted her position again.

"But why?"

Reaching into the food dish, she selected another piece of fruit. She didn't seem to care for it and tossed it aside.

"You said family is important," I reminded her.

"It is," she agreed without hesitation.

"And you said they are family," I continued.

"They are," she said with a slight nod.

"Then why?" I asked again.

"Because."

Reaching for another piece of fruit, she tossed it aside also. Mother seemed to conclude that she'd had enough to eat. She picked me up with one scoop of a long arm and tucked me up against her. Holding me close, she moved off toward the corner she favored. I knew that she planned to settle herself and have a nap. She would expect me to sleep as well. But I still wasn't satisfied with the answer I had been given. If family was important and the howlers and other creatures in our Primate House were family, then why were we not better acquainted with them?

"Why can't we?" I whimpered against Mother.

"There's no door," she said, appearing pleased with herself for coming up with the answer.

"But why? Can't the human-people make a door?"

"They don't want a door," said Mother

"Why?"

"It wouldn't be right."

I didn't understand that answer.

"Why?"

"We're different," she replied and settled herself in her corner. I knew that she would soon be asleep.

"But we're family," I reminded her.

"But different," she replied. She snuggled down, finding a more comfortable position. I knew that her eyes were already closing.

"I still don't understand . . ." I began, but she interrupted me.

"Ask your father," she replied sleepily. Pulling me closer against her furry chest, she patted my shoulder.

For some strange reason I suddenly felt sleepy. I was troubled with the question that had not been answered. I did need an answer. But it would have to wait. I needed some sleep. Later—later I would ask my father. He'd know. He was the Silver Back.

I sighed and cuddled close to Mother. "Tell me again," I said softly.

I did not have to explain what I meant to Mother. She knew exactly what I wanted to hear. For one moment her eyes opened wide. The expression on her face did not change but her eyes did. They began to twinkle. Then she held me even closer and began in a soft voice. "There was never a more exciting day at Roxbury Zoo than the day that you were born. Everyone had been waiting for you. Everyone. All of the family had been looking forward to having you join us. Ms. Evangeline kept asking me if it was 'time' yet. Big Sam, your father, kept offering me his slices of orange and asking if I felt well. Nick was always telling me to please hurry—and to be sure it was a boy. Mitsy nudged all of the choicest bits of fruit my way and Petunia even did her quarrelling quietly."

"Everyone in the family was waiting for you. Even the keepers were waiting for you. I heard them counting the days. They made sure I had plenty of nesting material and gave me special food to eat. They talked excitedly about your coming. 'It'll be a first,' they kept saying. 'A first for Roxbury Zoo.' They could hardly wait. 'It will be a special day,' they said."

"And sure enough—on the day that you were born, the whole zoo celebrated. The news traveled from cage to cage and home to home. The sparrows and mice and the human keepers saw to that. All of the animals and birds knew what the celebration was for. A brand new baby boy gorilla was born. It was the first baby gorilla for Roxbury Zoo. You were that baby. They even took pictures of you and Mrs. Sadie Sparrow said that you were on the front page of all of the newspapers in town. The humans flocked in to see you as soon as the doors opened each day. The little ones called out and pointed and the big

Roxbury Gazette

A First for Roxbury Zoo

ones laughed and chattered excitedly. You were the first baby gorilla they had ever seen."

"The zoo keepers had a big contest. They let the people suggest names. The winner was to get a full Season's Pass to the zoo. There was a big commotion about it. They finally decided on the name. It's posted over there on the big window. I couldn't see the name from this side so I had Tilly Mouse read it for me. It says, *Roxbury's latest addition. Roxie, our first baby Gorilla. He's Number One."*

Mother's eyes were closed and her voice was getting softer and softer. I knew that she was about ready to drop off to sleep. I nudged her and asked the same question that I always asked.

"Why did it say that?"

"Because," she answered and smacked her lips slightly. "Because."

"Why because?"

"Because that is what they named you."

"Who?"

She stirred slightly and snuggled herself in for her rest.

"I really don't know," she replied. "Just someone."

I shook her gently. "But that's not my name," I reminded her.

"I know." She yawned.

"Then why did they call me that?"

She pulled me closer against her and snuggled me into her dark fur. "Because," she said, and I knew she was almost asleep. "Because they didn't know that I had already named you Barnaby."

I grinned. I liked to be called Barnaby. I didn't care much for Roxie. But I did wish that they had it straight. I wished that the sign said, *Roxbury's newest member. Barnaby Gorilla.* Then everyone would know the truth. I wished with all of my heart that I had some way—or someone—to change the sign to what it really should be. Maybe—someday— but I was too sleepy to work on it now. I nestled close to Mother and let my eyes close. I grinned again to myself. It was nice to be so important. I was glad that everyone celebrated on the day that I was born. I was glad that I was Number One— and special.

Chapter Three

Outside

Mother said that we had about the nicest home that anyone could have. And it was. There was always plenty of good food here and there around our enclosure. It didn't take much effort on our part to seek it out. We knew that the task of food-finding was supposed to make us feel more at home and more on our own. We also knew that our cupboards were well-stocked by the human keepers. Still, if it entertained them to make us seek our food, we had no problem accommodating them. They fed us well, starting the day with our ape-juice. That was a treat that we all looked forward to each morning. I wasn't very old when I realized that it was a special part of our day.

Not only were we well-fed, but we had a comfortable and spacious concrete house with all of the things that made it homey, including a make-believe tree. We also had a large outdoor courtyard. I loved the out-of-doors. There was always so much to see. Above our heads the sky stretched on and on and large, real trees spread wide branches where leaves tumbled and danced in the afternoon breezes.

Overhead the birds seemed to be constantly on

the wing and all around were the whisperings and chatterings of other zoo animals. I loved it.

Of course there was also the 'crowd' as Mother called the multi-colored, constantly shifting group of humans that came and went and called and pointed. For the most part, Mother ignored them. In fact our whole family seemed to ignore them— all except Nick. He pretended to ignore them but, as I watched carefully, I was sure that he was very conscious of their presence. I was also sure that he 'performed' for the crowd just a little bit.

There were times when I wasn't sure which was the most interesting to watch—the crowd of people or Nick. The crowd was busy and colorful and continually changing. Still, after one had watched it for a while, it was rather predictable. But Nick? There was nothing predictable about Nick. Just when I thought that I had seen all of his tricks, he found something new to entertain the masses.

I had never seen anyone who could do such strange and interesting things with a ball. The keepers had placed a large blue rubber ball in our court. I guess they knew that young gorillas like Nick need something to do. We also had other toys like plastic buckets and an old bicycle tire. Nick found ways to climb in and out of the tire and bounce the rubber ball that were almost impossible to imagine. Everyone clapped and shouted and pointed at him, enjoying his games immensely.

Nick pretended that he didn't know what they were all hooting about but I saw him sneak a peek at the crowd every now and then.

I could hardly wait until I was old enough to do a little performing of my own. Mother still kept me quite close but I was given a bit more freedom than I'd had in the past. Still, I could often feel Mother's eye on me and knew that she was watching carefully to make sure that nothing happened to Roxbury Zoo's first gorilla baby.

I wasn't sure which I preferred. The out-of-doors where I could see the whole, wide, wonderful world or the inside where I could watch the antics of the howlers as they bounced off the sides of their cage and leaped from floor to ceiling. Or the chimps who chortled and ambled around their cage doing the funniest things and making the most outrageous remarks. When I sat and watched them, they would look at me in a friendly manner and blink back at me when I blinked at them.

I loved my world. There was always something going on, and so many things to see and hear. I could hardly wait until I was big enough to explore it on my own.

* * * * *

"Hey, Barn. Wanna have some fun?"

It was Nick who asked the question. He had taken to calling me Barn rather than Barnaby when he knew that my mother wasn't close enough to correct him. I looked over toward Mother who sat quietly being groomed by Mitsy. She was giving me more freedom now and I was loving every minute of it.

I turned back to Nick.

"Georgie thinks he's pretty hot stuff," he confided, nodding his head toward the home of the chimps.

I knew Georgie. He was an even bigger show-off than Nick. But he was fun, one had to admit that. And he was friendly. I rather liked Georgie.

"So-o?" I asked Nick hesitantly.

"So I think it's about time for someone to upstage him."

"Upstage?" I hadn't heard that word before.

"Yeah. Do him one better. Take away a little of his limelight. Get a few of his laughs."

I still didn't understand what Nick was talking about. I sat and looked at him, blinking my eyes and working my mouth.

"So-o?" I asked again.

"Well, we are gonna do it," he went on.

"We?" I looked over at Mother again. She seemed to be totally absorbed in her beauty routine. I shifted a bit nervously.

"I've got this new trick," said Nick in a confidential whisper. "Only it takes two."

I felt a tingle pass all through me. I had watched and admired Nick for a long time and now I was to be part of the action. I was flattered that he was actually inviting me to join him.

"See Georgie?" whispered Nick.

How could one miss Georgie? He was over in his cage with one of the food pans turned upside-down on his head. Occasionally he would reach up and thump the pan, making weird hooting noises with his lips all puckered and smacking. The crowd outside his cage loved it. They clapped and pointed and laughed and chattered. Georgie looked around to be sure that he was getting their full attention. Then, to add to his little show, he found a small stick and began to thump himself on his pan-covered head. It made an awful din but the crowd clapped all the louder. I could see Georgie's eyes twinkle as he glanced at Nick. He knew that Nick hated to see the crowd cheering him on.

Nick nudged me to bring my attention back to him.

"I've got this new trick," he reminded me. "It's never been done before."

I blinked. "Then how do you know you can do it?" I asked frankly.

Nick gave me a look of disdain. I knew that I shouldn't have asked the question.

"We can do it," he said. "The crowd loves a new trick." He cast a glance Georgie's way, "Georgie's been doing that same ol' trick for months."

I looked over at Georgie too. It might be an old trick but it was funny. The crowd always loved it.

I turned back to Nick. "So what are we gonna do?" I asked innocently.

"Swing," he answered. His eyes sparkled at the thought of it.

"Swing?" Without thinking about it, I turned to the howlers. They were the swingers. Right now the two young ones known as Swinger and Spindle were romping around in the highest branches, chasing one another in their own version of tag. I wasn't very big—or very bright—but I knew with certainty that

I couldn't do that.

"Swing," repeated Nick.

"I can't do that," I said before I could stop myself and nodded at the howlers. Just then Spindle leaped from the highest branch right over Swinger's head. He bounced off the side of the cage onto a lower branch, then right over his mother's head and up to a rope that stretched across the cage.

"Not like that," said Nick disgustedly. "We'll do it our own way."

I looked back at Nick.

"We can't," I insisted. "We don't have tails."

Mother had told me that was one of the advantages the howlers had when I had asked her why I couldn't swing from the ropes and branches.

"We don't need tails," huffed Nick. "I told you, we'll do it our own way."

"And how's that?" I asked sharply.

I should have had a bit more respect for Nick. After all, he was my elder. But I was special. All of the family thought so. I guess I was a little bit spoiled by all of the attention. So I stood right up to Nick as an equal rather than following his orders without question.

"See this tire?" He held the old bicycle tire up for me to see. I had seen it dozens of times. Nick had done almost everything imaginable with that old tire. But he hadn't swung.

I looked at the worn-out old tire and back at Nick, then nodded slowly.

"Well, we are gonna swing with it." The twinkle was back in his eyes again.

"How?" I asked suspiciously. I was still in doubt.

"Easy," said Nick. "We are gonna hang it from the highest branch up there and swing back and forth on it."

It didn't sound like much in comparison to what the howlers could do.

"How you gonna get it up there?" I asked simply.

"I'll climb up and hook it over," he said, quite confident of the fact that he could do it.

"And then . . .?" I asked him.

"Then I will take hold of it and swing back and forth."

It sounded pretty tame to me.

"That's all?" I asked him.

He gave me a disdainful look. "'Course not," he said. "That wouldn't even be worth looking at."

I looked up at the make-believe branch way over our head. It wouldn't be such an easy thing to do. Perhaps the crowd would be interested in watching it.

Nick's eyes followed mine. "Well," he conceded, "it might be a little interesting—but not nearly as interesting as what I have in mind."

"What're you gonna do?" I asked him.

"You," he said, pointing a finger at my chest. "You. That's where you come in."

I looked up again. I had never been to the top of our tree. Mother didn't like me to do much climbing. Truth was, I still wasn't very good at it. I began to shake my head.

"You won't need to go all the way to the top,"

Nick hurried to inform me. "Just up to that second big branch."

I waited to find out more about what he had in mind.

"I'll go up to the top and hook the tire over the big branch. Then I'll grab hold of it and swing down from it. You'll climb on that second branch and grab hold of my feet. Then we'll swing back and forth together. Like a trapeze."

"What's a trapeze?" I asked him.

"It's a . . ." He gave me another look of disgust and shrugged. "You'll see," he told me. "Just do as I say."

He sat there looking at our tree. I knew that he was trying to picture just how we'd look doing our little act.

"Maybe you should bring the ball," he mused. "That would add to the trick."

"The ball? How can I bring the ball?" I asked him irritably.

"Oh, come on, Barn!" he chided me. "Stop acting like a child."

"What will I do with the ball?" I asked him.

"Well, we'll join feet to swing and you can hold the ball in your hands. Then throw it into the pail when we swing over it."

"I couldn't hit the pail," I protested.

"Well, just throw it at the pail then," he said in exasperation. "Do something with it. Anything. I don't care—but we've got to do more than just swing."

"You handle the ball," I told him.

"Me? I have to hold the tire—and you. You couldn't hold me up there."

That was true. Nick was much bigger than I.

He turned to me again. "You ready?" he asked me.

I looked over at Mother. She seemed to have fallen asleep. Mitsy still continued the grooming.

I looked back at Nick and nodded. "But I don't know about the ball," I still argued.

"Well, find something else then," he said. He still sounded in a huff. "Something you can handle."

He emphasized the *you* as though he knew that there was very little that I could handle. I shrugged and went to look for something small in our cage that I could carry up the tree.

There wasn't much available. I finally decided on a banana that had been overlooked at lunch. I picked it up and followed Nick.

He was having more trouble than he had anticipated trying to get the tire up the tree. It seemed that he needed both of his hands for climbing. With one hand securely holding the tire, he would reach for a hold on the tree trunk and try to draw himself up; but each time he would come tumbling back down.

Then he would lean the tire against the tree, climb up and reach back down for it. But the next step he took would dislodge the tire again and it would go tumbling and thumping to the ground. I didn't think that he was ever going to make it. And then he seemed to get a good idea. He hung the tire around his neck and climbed with both hands. The tire bumped along over his shoulders but he was making some progress. He reached the first big limb and shuffled himself up onto it. The tire was awkward to work with and he tried to shift its weight around. The whole process unbalanced him and he began to slip. I was sure that he was going to come tumbling down but, at the very last moment, he managed to grab hold of the tree and hang on. The tire wasn't so lucky. It came tumbling down, bounced a couple times on the hard concrete floor, then rolled over to the side where it butted up against the broad back of my father.

He turned, his face a blank stare, and looked at the offending circle as though wondering how the inert piece of rubber had suddenly been given life. Then his eyes lifted to study Nick who still clutched the tree branch. He seemed to have his explanation. Nick was up to one of his shenanigans again. Father just blinked and reached back to rub at the spot where the tire had bumped him.

Nick breathed a sigh of relief when he realized that he was not going to be scolded. Then he made his way down from the tree and retrieved the tire again.

On his second try he made it all the way to the top. Then came the more difficult maneuver of climbing out on the limb and hooking the tire over the end of it. I held my breath as he tried time after time. Finally he managed to get the tire in place. He looked down at me and nodded. "Come on up," he said in a voice that was meant to be a whisper.

I saw his eyes travel to the glassed front of the

cage. Already a crowd was gathering. They had been observing Nick and his climb. Nick's eyes then went to the chimp's cage. Georgie had lost much of his crowd.

I began my climb shakily. I wasn't used to climbing, especially with a banana in one hand. Surely it would be smashed to pulp by the time I reached the second branch where I was to join Nick's little circus act. Could I possibly get that far? By the time I reached it, I was weak from the effort, either from exertion or nerves. I stopped to rest for a moment, trying hard to catch my breath and calm myself.

"There's nothing to it," Nick was saying above me. "All you have to do is grab my feet with your feet."

I looked up at him. How on earth was I to get my feet up to his?

"Why don't I just use my hands?" I protested.

"You have to hold the ball in your hands," he reminded me.

"I don't have a ball," I replied, a bit miffed. "You said to get what I can handle. Remember?"

He looked disgusted. "So what did you get?" he asked.

I held up the banana. He groaned.

"Not a banana. They'll think we're nuts."

I wouldn't have argued that point.

Suddenly he seemed to brighten. "Hey," he said, "peel it while we swing."

"Peel it?"

"Yeah. Peel it while we're swinging." Then as though getting a brilliant afterthought, he added,

"An' eat it."

Now I groaned.

"With your feet," he added quickly as though that would add a special effect. "Do it with your feet."

"How can I do it with my feet if I have to hang on to you?" I argued.

He seemed to consider that. "Well—hang on to me with your hands then," he agreed. "Peel the banana with your feet. An' eat it," he added, not wanting me to forget my orders.

I looked at the half-squashed banana in my hand and then reached down and placed it on the branch beside my foot. I'd have to pick it up at the last moment just before Nick swung me out on the tire.

"When I say 'go' you leap and grab my feet," Nick informed me.

"Leap?"

This little trick was getting trickier by the minute.

"You can leap," he said disgustedly. "I'll grab you."

I hated the very thought of it. I just knew that I would fall. The hard concrete looked a long way beneath me.

Nick had managed to get his tire swinging above my head. He was holding on tightly, his body extending down toward my tree limb but just beyond my reach. If I had to grab hold of his feet I would need to leap, there was no doubt about that.

I waited for the signal. Nick was swinging faster and faster and wider and wider. I reached out with my toes and grabbed the banana. I felt it squish. It wouldn't be fit to eat by the time I came to that part of the performance. I perched on the edge of the branch, tense and breathless.

"Go," I heard Nick hiss and I looked up to find his outstretched feet and leaped to grab at them.

By some miracle I was successful. I heard the crowd cheer wildly and I knew with satisfaction that we were being watched.

Nick picked up momentum. I knew that he had heard the crowd as well. He was performing to the maximum. For one moment I felt fear ripple up my spine. I was afraid that Nick would get carried away with all of the attention and toss me into the air or some such thing.

We were swinging gently back and forth when I heard Nick hiss again. "Peel the banana," he instructed me.

I had quite forgotten the poor banana that I clutched in the toes of one foot. But with Nick's words I reached my other foot toward it, concentrating hard on getting my feet together and getting the toes to do the job set out for them. I finally managed to get a break in the peel so that I could begin to strip the banana.

"Eat it," ordered Nick.

We were swinging even higher now. It might have been fun had I not been so nervous. I wished that Nick could have been content to just swing.

At last I managed to get my foot up high enough to get one bite of banana into my mouth. I got some peel along with it and I didn't care much for the taste of that. The rest of the banana went tumbling down to the floor beneath us. I heard it land with

a dull thud and hoped that Nick didn't realize what had happened.

The crowd was cheering wildly. Georgie was looking our way with a grumpy glare. I began to catch a bit of Nick's spirit. We had done it. We had outperformed the choice performers. We had outshone the chimps.

Just when I was beginning to feel smug about our whole little act, something went wrong. I'm not sure what happened but I heard Nick cry out and then I felt myself falling through the air. I had lost my hold on Nick's feet. He would not have been able to save me anyway as he seemed to be falling right along with me. Frantically, I began to reach out with both my fingers and my toes, clutching for something to cling to.

There wasn't anything to grab onto but handfuls of air but I continued to clutch and grab. I was braced for the smack against our concrete floor when my stretching, clutching hand found something solid to grasp. I closed my fingers tightly and clung for all I was worth.

A loud screech made me open my eyes to see what had stopped my fall. It was Petunia, her eyes wild, her mouth wide open in fear and protest. I was clinging to her with both hands and both feet. One set of fingers was tightly clutching the fur on the top of her head. The other arm was wrapped around her neck with my hand to her upper arm. One set of toes dug sharply into her right side and the other was threatening to pull the fur from the middle of her back.

She grunted, then began to shriek as she realized what had suddenly landed on her from above.

"Your child," she screamed toward the spot where my mother had been relaxing. Mother was not relaxing now. She was sitting bolt upright, her eyes wide with horror and fright. Perhaps I had cried out as I had fallen from the air. I didn't know. I only knew that Mother was poised for fight or rescue as necessary. I could see it in her eyes.

Mother moved quickly forward and began to disentangle my fingers and toes from Petunia's fur.

"He attacked me," Petunia was screaming. "He flung himself right at me in the most . . . most . . ." She didn't seem to be able to find words to express her outrage.

"He fell," said Mother. "He fell from the tree."

"He viciously attacked me," insisted Petunia.

Mother was still shaking her head. She drew me to herself and cradled me close. I was trembling violently from my terrible fright.

"He fell from the tree," Mother insisted. She was sounding much calmer now that she knew that I was still in one piece.

"Well, what was he doing in the tree anyway?" Petunia flung at Mother as she began to brush and smooth her fur coat.

Mother seemed to consider that for a moment and then she answered evenly, her eyes traveling toward the tree that I had just descended from so ungracefully, "I've no idea."

My eyes traveled upward as well. There sat Nick. He had managed to catch onto the last branch of the tree. He still sat there, blinking his eyes in unbelief. The old rubber tire was wrapped around his neck. He seemed unable to move—or perhaps he wasn't sure if he dared to come down. Petunia was still raging and screaming about undisciplined young who pounced on one unexpectedly from above, as she scurried off to her own corner to pout.

Old Ms. Evangeline squinted through watery eyes but I was sure that she had seen the whole proceedings. In fact, I wondered if I didn't see her smile just a bit.

Chapter Four

Neighbors

For the next several days I stayed away from Nick. I was not going to be his partner in another antic. Even though we had received thunderous applause and lots of hoots and laughter from the humans who gathered to watch our act, I wasn't showman enough to risk my life and limb for the cause.

Nick kept to himself. Perhaps our little experience shook him up more than he wished to admit. I noticed that he stayed away from the right side of our cage. It seemed that he didn't wish to be heckled by Georgie.

Georgie had gone back to stealing the show. He was acting out his little charades with the feeding dishes again—but he added a new twist. Now, instead of just hitting himself over the head with the little stick, he was climbing his little tree and pretending to fall while beating on the pan. Both Nick and I knew that he was having fun at our expense. Suddenly, I wasn't overly fond of Georgie.

There was another young chimp in the neighboring cage who was most friendly. Her name was Jenny Lou and she always came to talk with me when I was on that side of our enclosure. She was never pert or sassy and never teased or ridiculed. I liked Jenny Lou. I noticed that she even sat and visited with the mice who ran in and out helping themselves to the leftovers in the food basins. And she talked to the sparrows as well, wishing them a good day and asking them about the latest brood they had hatched and how they were doing. She was a nice girl, Jenny Lou.

Much of her time seemed to be taken trying to keep an eye on the youngest member of the chimp family. He was about my size but older. Mother said that I would soon pass him in size. Mother was always silently comparing the two of us. I knew that she was proud that I was already as big as he was. But I had to admit that he was more sure of what to do with his arms and legs than I was.

His name was Minx. Many times I wished that we could share a cage. I was sure that he would be a wonderful playmate. Minx was always getting into things from which Jenny Lou had to rescue him. But it always looked like fun.

The other youngster in the cage next door was Ginger. She usually ignored us. In fact, she seemed to be interested mainly in herself. She was continually primping or asking to be groomed. Mother didn't pay much attention to Ginger but I heard Petunia say plenty about the snooty young chimp next door. "Miss Goody-Goody" Petunia called her or "Her Royal Highness" and at times she even changed it to "Her Spoiled Highness." I had noticed that Petunia could put on just as many airs as Ginger when she had a mind to. The two seemed to take a good

deal of pleasure in snubbing one another through the partition of our cages.

There was one thing about the chimps that I deeply admired. They could stand right up and walk on their two hind legs. They often dropped down and made use of their arms too but, if they wished or if they had their hands filled with something, then they'd just stand up and walk. I tried it over and over but I never could get it to work for me.

The howlers were too busy to be good neighbors. But then, they were not bad neighbors. They simply did not take time from their jumping and leaping and swinging to pay much attention to us. They didn't even pay attention to the crowd that gathered in front of their glass section and 'ohhed' and 'ahhed' over their acrobatics.

Swinger or Spindle or Hardy did call out a greeting now and then as they went flying past from branch to rope or rope to wall, but there was never time for a real conversation.

I didn't mind. I liked to just sit and watch them. I couldn't imagine what it would be like to be able to do the extraordinary things that they were able to do.

"Why can't we do that?" I asked Mother until she was tired of hearing it.

Her only answer seemed to be that we didn't have tails. Oh, how I wished that I had a tail so that I could have enjoyed the activity of the howlers. I even started dreaming about it.

* * * * *

Mother called me from my play with the blue rubber ball and I went to her as I had been taught.

"We're going out," she said in answer to the question that she must have read in my eyes.

I loved to go out but as yet I was not allowed to go unless Mother was going. I grabbed unto Mother's fur and swung myself up unto her back. I had to remember to duck as we passed out of the door that led to the outside courtyard.

It was a beautiful day. The sun was shaded by scurrying clouds and the wind blew furiously through the trees, tossing the branches and making the leaves dance and sing. Something within me responded to the wildness of the weather. Perhaps it had something to do with the fact that Mother said we were really creatures of the wild—quite capable of caring for our own needs.

For whatever reason, I loved the tempestuous weather. I think Mother felt that way about it too. She always went out on the fiercely windy days. There she would sit on her favorite rock in the big courtyard and let the wind blow fully into her face, parting her fur and tugging at her coat.

On such days, Petunia never went out-of-doors. "Not fit weather for beast, bird or bluegill," she would stew.

The first time I heard her make that comment, I turned to Mother. "What's a bluegill?" I asked her.

"A fish," she replied off-handedly.

"What's a fish?" I continued.

She looked thoughtful for a few minutes as though

wondering just how to answer my question.

"They swim," she said at last.

"Swim? What's swim?"

She was really puzzled then. At length she said slowly, "They live in water."

I had looked over at the trickle of water that continually ran down from the little pipe along one wall of our cage. It disappeared to some unseen place below that Father called the 'drain.'

"In there?" I asked Mother.

"Not in there. In big water."

"Where?" I asked. Then I thought of the moat around our outside court. It had water—and it was big water. "In the moat?" I asked.

"No, not in the moat," she said, shaking her head.

"Then where?" I insisted.

Mother got up from where she had been sitting. "Come," she said. "It's almost time for dinner."

I hadn't been satisfied with her non-answer and every time that I came near water, I looked for the fish. So far I had seen nothing.

This day as I sat near mother, feeling the wind pulling at my fur and tickling my ears, I thought again of the fish and wondered when I would ever be able to see them for myself.

"Do you know fish?" I asked Mother suddenly.

She turned to study me for a moment, then she nodded her head slowly. "I've seen them," she answered, "though I haven't met any personally."

"Where?" I asked, not willing to let it go.

"In the water," she answered rather thoughtlessly.

"What water?"

She did not answer.

"What water?" I insisted, tugging on her coat.

She reached out and drew me close. At times she seemed to forget that I was no longer her tiny one. I was growing up, though I still depended on her much more than I liked to admit.

"At the zoo. The one where I lived before I came here. We had them in our moat there."

"You lived in another zoo?" I had never heard that before.

Mother nodded.

"Where?" I asked her.

"Many miles from here. Somewhere. I'm not sure where."

"What was it like? Do you . . .?"

"My mother is there," she answered me and there was a strange wistfulness in her voice.

I couldn't imagine what it would be like to live somewhere separate from my mother. Suddenly I was glad to be held tightly up against her. I cuddled in closer and wrapped my fingers into the hair on her chest. I hoped with all of my heart that I would never, ever, ever have to know what it would be like to live without my mother.

* * * * *

Father came out to join us. He sat down with his big, broad back to the wind and watched the few humans who braved the wind to stand and stare at the gorillas. Father wasn't one to do much talking but I heard him speak to Mother now.

"Look at them," he said and there was a hint of laughter in his voice. "They have to hold their fur-skin on with both hands."

I looked at the people. Sure enough. Many of them were clutching tightly to their colorful skins.

"What would happen?" I dared to ask. "What would happen if they let go?"

Father shrugged his shoulders and rocked back and forth gently. "I've no idea," he responded. "No idea."

"I wish they wouldn't," I found myself saying. "I wish they wouldn't hold on so tight. I wish they'd let go. I'd like to see . . ."

Just then a gust of wind whipped around the corner of the building next to ours and swept over the crowd of onlookers. Hands clutched and grabbed and things flapped and waved in the wind. What a commotion there was. But I was disappointed. With all of their scurrying and grabbing they had all managed to hang on to their skins. And then the strangest thing happened. Suddenly the wind lifted the top off the head of one of the humans leaning over our fence, carried it right over our moat, and deposited it in our yard. I had never seen anything like it. I reached up to my own head to make sure that I still had all of my fur-skin. I did.

Then I looked back at the human. He didn't seem to be in any pain—but that whole piece of his head was missing. It lay in our courtyard, gently rocking back and forth as the wind continued to play with it.

Father left our side and made his way slowly down the slope toward it. He picked it off the ground and looked at it, turning it this way and that way in his big hands. Then he sniffed at it. He turned it around and around again. Next he lifted it to his lips and nibbled at it, though he didn't really take a bite. I knew that he wasn't planning to eat it but was just checking it out.

When he had studied it and turned it over and over, he crossed to a rock on the side of the slope and sat down, the funny bit of the human's top still in his hands. He surveyed the crowd as though studying just where the piece belonged on one's anatomy. Then he reached up and pushed the top of the human's head-part right down over his own head. It looked funny sitting up there on his furry brow. One side of the brim dipped down and covered one of his eyes. He reached up and thumped it down a little further. The small crowd around the court began to laugh and clap. They seemed to think the whole thing was terribly amusing. I guess they had never seen a gorilla wearing a human's top before. Even Mother's eyes took on a twinkle. She must have thought Father looked a bit comical too.

Then Father stood up slowly from his rock seat, stretched to his full height and lifted his furry fists to beat a rapid drum-roll on his broad chest. The crowd roared even louder.

Father did not even glance their way but turned and ambled across the courtyard and through the entrance door into our den, the human piece still crookedly perched on one side of his head.

I was very curious about the strange top and followed quickly after Father in order to get a good look at it.

Father allowed me to poke at it and even to sniff it and nibble at it as he had done but he did not allow me to remove it from his head.

It was a strange thing. Not furry or hairy at all and it had this funny brim-part that dipped down to one side, though Father had rearranged the shape of it with all his pounding and pommelling.

When the day ended and we turned to our beds for the night, Father still had the top. Now and then he pulled it off and studied it again. But he always smacked it back on the top of his head and grunted a satisfied grunt. I saw him reach up and check on it just before he went to sleep. I knew that he liked it but I couldn't quite figure out why.

Chapter Five

More Nick Hi-Jinks

I had often seen the gibbons in one of the enclosures across the way from us. They were an energetic group that seemed to spend even more time flying through the air than the howlers. But they were harder for us to see, especially at the times when the doors were open and the crowds passed between our cages.

The crowds had left to go wherever they go at the end of the day and the human keepers had closed the doors. I guess they had gone off too, for things were quiet. That is, there was no noise except the cries and screams and hoots and calls from the primates.

It was noisy enough, I can tell you that. The howlers were particularly noisy. I wondered if something dreadful was taking place in their cage or if they were just excited. They often made a big fuss for no apparent reason.

Across from us and to our left was a very strange family. Mother insisted that they were our relatives but I could scarcely believe it. I mean, they looked so different. The first time that I had seen them, I wondered what they were doing in our world.

"They're family," Mother had said.

I stared at them. "Are you sure?" I had asked in doubt.

"I'm sure," she answered. "They are the baboons. Cousins."

I looked at them with their strange long noses. "They sure are funny looking," I told Mother.

"No one is funny looking," replied Mother gently. "Just different."

I may not have agreed but I didn't dare to argue.

I looked over at the baboon cage now. I still thought that they looked awfully funny. They were adding to the noise of all of the other primates in their own strange way.

Petunia was sitting over in her corner, her hands over her ears. There was a frown on her face. I could hear her mumbling to herself—something about the fact that such ridiculous carrying-on should not be tolerated. I assumed she was speaking of the noise. The howlers sounded as if they were leading some sort of rebellion.

But it was the gibbons who had drawn my attention. I stared at them open-mouthed.

After watching the howlers from day to day, the jumping and swinging of the gibbons should not have taken me by surprise. They certainly looked different from the howlers. They seemed to be all long, lanky legs and string-bean arms. Father said that if you stuffed half a dozen of them in a stew pot, you'd still have nothing but bones.

I wasn't sure what Father meant. I had no idea

what a stew pot was or what one did with it.

As I watched the gibbons float and swing, I suddenly noticed something else about them. I stared, unable to believe my own eyes.

"Nick," I cried without even turning around to see where he was. "Nick. Look!"

I don't know where he had been or what he had been doing but he was soon by my side, a small twig from one of the outside trees held in one hand.

"Look!" I said again, excitedly.

"At what?" he asked, sitting down beside me.

"The gibbons. There."

He followed my instructions. I could tell by the turn of his head. But he didn't seem to get nearly as excited as I was.

"Look at them swing and leap," I continued breathlessly.

"So?" he asked with a shrug. "They do that all the time."

"But how?" I asked, turning to him excitedly. "They don't have tails. Mother said you need a tail to jump like that."

"Not gibbons," said Nick, shaking his head. "I've seen them do that over and over and I haven't seen one of them with a tail yet."

I reached out and pushed at Nick's shoulder. He didn't seem to be getting the point at all.

"Then why can't we?" I asked him. "If they don't need a tail to do it, why can't we?"

Nick looked at me, his eyes growing big. He seemed to be thinking about it. Then he cast a glance toward the grown-ups who stretched out lazily about the cage—except for Petunia who still sat pouting in the corner and Ms. Evangeline who rested, eyes closed, in her own special spot.

"Maybe they just don't want us to know," Nick said in a hoarse whisper. "Maybe we could do it if we tried."

I nodded and cast a glance toward my mother and father. Had they been keeping secrets from me? And why?

We exchanged glances again and then Nick nodded his head toward the door that led to the outside court-yard. I knew what he meant.

He led the way and I followed quietly, so as not to draw the attention of the older family members.

It was quiet in the court. Only the sounds of other creatures that belonged to the zoo reached us across the still, evening air. A soft glow put a blush on the western sky. The fragrance of the flower beds across the park wafted to us on the gentle breeze. Nearby the birds were noisily gossiping about the events of the day before tucking in for the night. I loved this time of the day. I could have just sat right down and enjoyed it but Nick was chattering at me excitedly.

I turned to him and then remembered why we had left the cage and come to the court.

"We'll practice out here in that big tree," he said, still whispering. "As soon as we get practiced up, we'll put on a show for 'em. As a surprise."

I felt excitement course through me. I could hardly wait. I had always imagined how much fun it must be to swing about from limb to limb and rope to rope. Well, we didn't have any ropes strung across the courtyard but we did have some nice tree branches. We'd practice on those and when the human keepers saw how good we were, I was sure that they would string up some ropes for us, too.

"I think we should try it one at a time so that the other fella can keep an eye on things and give advice on form an' such," said Nick.

I nodded. I wasn't sure what he meant by form and keeping an eye on it but it sounded wise enough.

"So who goes first?" he continued.

I looked up into the tree. I was anxious to give it a try.

"Well, as the oldest . . ." he began.

"But I saw the gibbons," I cut in. "You hadn't even noticed that they didn't have tails."

"Did too," he argued with me. "Just never paid much attention to it, that's all."

"Well, I did. I thought about us."

"But you still didn't think about practicing," he argued further.

I still thought that I should get the credit for my discovery but it was getting late. I was afraid that Mother might suddenly start looking for me and I'd have to go in without getting a chance to try at all.

"I guess you can go first," I said condescendingly. "It was your idea. Sort of." There was no way that I was going to give him all the credit.

He nodded and moved forward, then stopped and turned suddenly. "Oh, go ahead," he said. "You're the youngest."

I didn't like to be reminded about that. The truth

was, as the younger I really was supposed to look up to Nick. I didn't feel like looking up to Nick. I was the one who'd had my picture on the front of the town newspaper. I was the one that the humans flocked to the zoo to see.

But I put all of that aside as I moved eagerly toward the big tree with its spreading branches. I would go first.

Nick moved right along with me. "Climb up onto that branch up there—that big one that's in the clear—and then jump to that one over there and swing around to that one," he said, hurriedly pointing out each of the branches as he spoke of them.

I could hardly wait to get up the tree. My whole body shook with anticipation. I had waited and dreamed of this day. I had thought that it was a dream that would never come true just because I had no tail. But now, now I was about to make my first jump. I would fly through the air like the howlers. No—like the gibbons. Swinging and leaping through the branches. It didn't matter one bit that I didn't have a tail.

I positioned myself carefully on the branch that Nick had selected and prepared myself for the thrill of a lifetime. Then I took a deep breath and leaped through the air anticipating the feeling of soaring.

But something went all wrong. My leap across to the branch I had selected was way short of my goal. I reached awkwardly with short, clutching arms but there was nothing to grab on to. With a sickening feeling, I realized that my soaring was taking me straight down, and the ground seemed to be coming up to meet me at an awfully fast pace.

"Stop," screamed Nick. "Hang on."

It sounded like wonderful advice but I wondered just what he expected me to hang on to.

And then I hit the ground. I would never have believed how hard earth could be. It knocked all the wind from me and I just lay there, rolling slightly, fighting hard to try to get some air back into my lungs.

I knew Nick was still there. I could hear his excited screaming and sensed that he was by my side, jumping up and down as his shrieks filled the evening air.

A real commotion followed. I don't know who reached me first—Father or Mother. But I do know that soon they were both bending over me, asking questions that I didn't have the breath to answer and shaking me excitedly. Mitsy had joined them, anxiously asking questions of her own and even Petunia was hovering near-by, wringing her hands and grunting her protests over the incident.

At last I was able to catch my breath and I used it to set up a howl that could be heard for a long way. Mother snatched me up and cuddled me, with comforting little 'tut-tuts,' asking what happened and how was I hurt and where did it hurt all in one quick breath.

I took full advantage of the opportunity to wail. It was rather pleasant to get all the attention. Even elderly Ms. Evangeline had come from her spot in the corner of our enclosure to look at me tenderly with watery eyes and pat me gently with her gnarled, bony fingers.

Mother tried to hush me with comforting grunts and chortles but I had no intention of stopping the noise until I was good and ready. Besides, I still hurt from the fall. It had been a long way down and the ground was much harder than I had imagined.

When I finally slowed down to a whimper, Mother rocked me gently back and forth, patted my shoulder, and soothed me with stubby, leathery fingers.

"Whatever happened?" she asked again. I had dreaded the question. I wasn't sure how I should answer.

At last I sobbed out my reply. "I fell from the tree," I admitted.

"But why? You know how to hold on tightly. I've shown you. Your father has . . ." I didn't want to admit that I hadn't even tried to hold on tightly. I looked around for Nick. He was nowhere to be seen.

I didn't wish to answer Mother's question so I did the only thing I knew to do. I started to cry noisily again.

Mother seemed to forget the question then. She cuddled me close and then carried me back to our cozy nest. "Sh-h," she comforted me. "Sh-h. You'll be alright. Nothing is broken. You'll be miserably sore for a few days—but you'll be alright."

I snuggled close to Mother. If she was willing to forget her question, I was willing to stop crying. I sniffled and pushed in more tightly against her. I still hadn't spotted Nick.

"I should have let him go first," I told myself. "I should have let him smack the hard ground. It

was his dumb idea."

It had all seemed like such a good plan. The gibbons had no tails. Yet they could do it.

I buried my face against Mother and wrapped my fingers in her long hairy fur. Even I was smart enough to know now that tails were not the answer. There was no way that I, Barnaby Gorilla, would ever be able to soar through the air like a gibbon. No way.

* * * * *

It took several days before all of the aches and pains left my body. I took full advantage of my invalid state. Mother waited on me hand and foot. Even Father allowed me freedoms that he had not allowed in the past. Of course Mitsy fussed over me something awful. And even though Petunia did not fuss, she didn't fret quite as much either. And Ms. Evangeline reached out and patted me whenever I came near enough for her to reach me, and said things like, "Poor little precious," and "Blessed little darlin'." It was all quite heady.

But all good things must end, they say. I wasn't sure just when to end this good thing. I would have loved to go on and on soaking in all of the special attention—but there was one problem. As long as I played the part of the invalid, I also had to curtail some of my fun. It was hard to balance the two pleasures, but at length I decided that I'd had enough coddling and would welcome more independence again. I informed Mother that I was feeling much better and looked around for Nick.

Chapter Six

Petunia

Petunia was particularly testy. It seemed to me that she fretted and stewed about everything that went on around us. She always tried to be first at mealtime and still she screamed that she wasn't getting her rightful share or the humans weren't bringing decent food or it was too old, too fresh, too warm or too cold. I got awfully tired of her pickiness. I even said so to Mother but she patted me gently and told me to be patient—that often things were not as they seemed and that sometimes one did not understand the pain of others.

I looked over at Petunia. I couldn't see that there was anything wrong with her.

It was Mitsy who was changing. Day by day she seemed to be getting plumper and plumper. I also noticed that she was treated with some sort of favor. Father gave her his orange portions at times and Mother seemed to hover over her in a protective fashion, making sure that she wasn't sitting in a draft or uncomfortable as she slept. It was all very strange to me. I didn't like the unusual feeling of tension that was in the air.

I tried to talk to Mother about it but she didn't

seem to understand my questions. I guess that wasn't Mother's fault. I couldn't really express what I was trying to say and so asked round-about questions instead. If I would have come right out and asked, "Why is everyone fussing over Mitsy?" or "Why is Petunia in such a foul mood?" I may have gotten some answers. Instead I asked things like, "Is Mitsy mad at me?" Or, "Why should I have to wait for Petunia to eat first?" Mother had a tendency to look at me with a blank expression on her face, then brush the question aside as though that was just the way things were. It was no explanation at all.

It was Nick who informed me of what was really going on.

We had been watching some ants in one corner of the courtyard one lazy summer day. They were busy little fellows, scurrying around with loads in their mouths bigger than what they, themselves, were. We teased them a little by putting small stones or pieces of sticks in their pathway. They always found ways to get around our barriers and just kept right on going.

From across the courtyard came the angry cry of Petunia. There was dirt on her favorite sitting-spot. It was likely the wind that had put it there but Petunia was sure that someone had done it maliciously. She screamed her anger and Father went over to wipe the spot clean and try to placate her.

I turned to Nick. The ants were forgotten.

"What's wrong with her anyway? She screams about everything."

Nick shrugged. "I dunno," he said.

That didn't answer my question.

I turned back to the ants.

I stuck a little piece of stick in the path of a scurrying ant whose load was so big he had to carry it backwards. He bumped into the stick just as Nick said, "I think she's just mad."

"Mad?"

That really didn't sound too insightful. Sure Petunia was mad. She was always mad about something.

I glanced her way. Father had managed to get her settled. He sat beside her quietly, the expression on his face as calm as ever.

"She's always mad," I said with emphasis.

Nick glanced at Petunia.

"I don't mean mad about the dirt—or mad about the food—I mean deep-down-inside mad."

I looked at Nick. What was he talking about?

"Sometimes the screamin' and yellin' isn't really about what is botherin'," Nick said knowingly.

"What do you mean?" I asked, casting another glance at Petunia.

"I think she feels left out," said Nick.

"Left out?"

"I don't think she feels special."

I frowned. I still couldn't figure out what Nick was trying to say.

"She doesn't get attention unless she screams. At least, she doesn't get as much attention as she wants," Nick went on.

"What do you mean?" I asked again.

Nick looked at me and heaved a sigh. It was as

though he was saying, "Boy, are you dumb," or "When are you ever gonna grow up?"

"Look," said Nick. "Your pa gets lots of attention because he's big. He's the boss. He's King. Okay?"

I nodded. My father got lots of attention alright. He was groomed and combed and respected.

"Ms. Evangeline gets attention because she's old an' wise and was . . . well, she's kinda nice," he finished lamely.

I nodded again.

"Your ma gets attention because she has you," said Nick bluntly.

I felt my chest swell a bit. I had really given my mother reason to be proud.

"I get attention because . . ." Nick stopped and cocked his head to the side. I could see his eyes start to twinkle. "Because I earn it," he said with bravado. "I'm young and . . . a little . . . shall we say mischievous. Okay, I'll admit it. I like attention. And I like experiencing life."

He sounded quite smug about it and suddenly I felt like giving him a good shove to bring him down to size.

"And Mitsy gets special attention because she's gonna have a baby," went on Nick very matter-of-factly.

My head came up.

"A baby?"

"Sure. Didn't you know?"

I shook my head. "No," I said. "I didn't know."

"Well, what'd you think . . .?"

I looked away and shrugged. "I dunno," I managed. "I dunno."

I felt a funny little chill creep up my spine and send shivers through my whole body. I wanted to ask Nick when this would take place but I didn't. I looked over at Petunia again. She was all huddled up as though the wind was blowing on her with a cold breath and her face wore the scowl that it always carried.

"So," I managed to say to Nick. "What's all that got to do with her?"

"Well," said Nick and he pulled himself up to his full height as we sat there on the ground. He seemed to puff out his chest a bit. "She doesn't have anything to get herself attention. That is, nothin' but her screamin' and complainin'."

I frowned as I thought about it.

"You really think . . .?"

"That's what I think," said Nick. I knew the way he said it that he figured I should believe whatever he had thought out.

"Sounds kinda weird," I argued.

"It is weird," Nick flung back at me. "Creatures are weird."

I looked at Petunia all wrapped up in herself. I couldn't argue with that point.

"So," I said at last. "Do we just have to put up with her screamin'?"

"I guess so," responded Nick. Then he stopped and thought for a moment. "Unless we can come up with some way to make Petunia feel noticed."

"Noticed?"

Somehow, coming from Nick, that word sounded dangerous.

I looked at him. He was derailing another little line of ants.

"Noticed, how?" I asked, unconsciously lowering my voice. The thought held a bit of promise.

Nick looked up at me and his eyes were twinkling. He lowered his head as he spoke as though fearing that someone from across the courtyard might read his lips if they were looking our way.

"The way I see it," he said, flashing an anxious look about us, "she's gonna scream anyway. We might as well have some fun out of it."

It sounded sane enough to me.

"So," I prompted Nick, my pulse beginning to beat just a bit faster.

"Well, I don't quite have it figured out yet," Nick said, disappointing me, "but I'm workin' on it."

The last words made me feel better. If Nick was working on it, something was sure to happen.

"When . . ." I began but Nick stopped me with a nod of his head and a knowing look.

"I'll let you know," he said as he got up from the ground, deserted the ants, and went to look for something more exciting to do.

I followed him.

There wasn't much going on around the courtyard. Petunia still sat, scowl-faced on her special spot. Father sat off to the side of her, distractedly chewing on a piece of branch the humans had left with us.

A few of the bright-skinned onlookers leaned over

the wall-fence and called across the moat as they pointed fingers and chatted in some strange-sounding language of their own. Apart from one young one who looked like he might be amusing, I found them of little interest.

I guess Nick felt the same for, after scanning the whole area, he turned to the entrance door and nodded his head. Without a word I followed him in.

Mother was sitting in the middle of our room carefully grooming Mitsy. I cast a quick glance at both of them. So that was what it was all about? Mitsy was going to have a baby. I still didn't understand why the whole family should be fussing over her just on that account. After all . . .

I looked more closely at Mitsy and the strange little feeling began to run up my spine again. I was the baby here. What right did Mitsy have to go and get another one?

Nick was nudging me and demanding my attention.

"Look at those gibbons."

I didn't really want to look at the gibbons. I hadn't enjoyed watching them ever since I had tried to do their stunts and knocked the wind out of myself. It just didn't seem fair that they could fly about like that without tails—when I had to be content to amble along the ground. Oh, I could climb well enough, but I sure couldn't swing through the trees.

I looked over at the gibbons. I had never seen such acrobatics. I guess the small crowd gathered in front of their cage encouraged their showing off.

The crowd was laughing and one little one in bright red skin was jumping up and down and clapping her hands as she watched.

I found the humans more interesting to watch than the gibbons. I couldn't do what the gibbons could do. I'd already found that out the hard way but I figured that I might be able to do some of the tricks that the humans did.

And then just as I watched, a big human reached down to a little human and started to peel part of her skin right off. First she slipped out one arm, then the other arm. She took the whole bright blue piece right off her arms, chest, and back. There was more skin underneath—just as though it came in layers. The underneath part was green. I stared open-mouthed. How did she ever do that? It seemed to come off easily. The big human took the skin-part and tossed it rather carelessly in a little cart that she was pushing and the small human kept right on watching the antics of the gibbons.

I looked down at my own body. I tugged a bit at the hair on my chest. It seemed solidly attached. I picked at the hair on my arms. Nothing wanted to move. I tried the other arm. It wouldn't budge there either. I looked back at the small human. There she was in her green skin. The blue skin-part still lay across the cart.

I turned away, shaking my head. "How in the world did she do that?" I wondered aloud. It was even trickier than swinging through the branches and ropes like the gibbons.

I sat down in the corner and went back to pulling and tugging at my own firmly attached fur. It wouldn't give. I guess I was just stuck in the same old color. I couldn't swing and I couldn't change skin-parts either.

Chapter Seven

The Rope

The next day Nick came to find me, dragging a piece of something behind him. It wasn't a tree limb—at least it didn't look like one to me. It wasn't stiff enough. It flipped and flopped all over.

"What's that" I asked him curiously.

"A rope," he answered, giving his wrist a flick that made the strange thing writhe on the ground.

"You gonna eat it?" I asked him.

He shook his head. "Doesn't even taste good," he answered and I supposed from his words that he had already tried it.

"Where'd you get it?" I asked him next.

"Georgie."

"Georgie gave you that?"

Nick hesitated. "Well," he said, "he didn't exactly give it to me."

I looked up at his face. His eyes were twinkling again.

"What do you mean?" I asked quickly.

"I sorta . . . took it," said Nick and he looked quite smug about it.

"Took it?"

"Yeah," Nick jerked his head toward the cage

where the chimps lived. "He had it sorta tied to the side of the cage. I worked it through the mesh with my fingers."

"Does he know it's gone?" I asked casting a nervous glance toward the chimps.

"Not yet," said Nick, "but I'm sure he'll discover it before long."

I shuffled around, licking my lips and looking toward the chimps. I wondered if Georgie would be upset to discover his rope missing.

"What does he do with that thing?" I asked Nick, swatting at the piece of rope.

"I saw him playing with it. Draggin' it around. Wrappin' it around things," said Nick and shrugged a shoulder again. "I dunno," he finished lamely.

I looked over at the chimp cage again, then back at Nick. "So what you gonna do with it?" I asked him.

"I dunno," he answered. "I'll think of somethin'."

"You better not let Georgie see that you have it," I cautioned.

"I'm not worried 'bout Georgie," said Nick with a nervous glance over his shoulder.

I looked around.

"What?" I asked him.

"Yer ma," he said. "If she sees it she'll make me give it back."

"Why?"

"'Cause. She says that . . . that we are never to take what belongs to another. She thinks that's . . . that's wrong or something."

I'd heard my mother say that too. Many times.

"Gets a fellow in trouble," I said to Nick, repeating my mother's words.

"What kinda trouble could one get in, just for takin' an old worn-out piece of rope?" asked Nick rather huffily.

"I dunno," I answered, "but Mother says . . ."

"I know what she says," responded Nick. "She's been tellin' me that since I was a kid."

Nick's words piqued my curiosity. I had often wondered, but never asked, what the strange connection was between Nick and my mother. She always seemed to have one eye on him, watching that he didn't get into too much trouble, scolding him gently when he went a bit too far, even holding him on those rare occasions when he wished to be cuddled.

I looked at Nick now. "What's the deal between you and my mother?" I asked him directly.

"What do you mean?" he asked.

"Well, I just . . . just . . . I've noticed that she . . . she sorta looks out for you."

"All gorillas look out for all family members," he answered.

That was true. I knew that. But that still didn't explain the fact that Mother seemed to have a special concern for Nick.

"But she . . .? You . . .?"

"I guess she sorta feels like a ma to me." answered Nick.

"A ma?"

"Yeah."

"Why?" My question was blunt. Direct. I didn't

really want my mother to be a ma to anyone else.

"'Cause. 'Cause I lost my own ma. They sent me here with your ma."

"Who sent you?"

"I dunno. The other zoo. Where your ma came from. I dunno. I was pretty little yet."

I was beginning to understand. Then suddenly I wondered if Nick had made headlines as I had made headlines.

"Were you born at the zoo?" I asked quickly.

"I dunno. No . . . no, your ma said I was born somewhere else. I dunno. I never paid much attention. What does it matter anyway?" He shrugged his shoulders again and turned his attention back to the rope he held in his hand.

I breathed a sigh of relief. I was glad that he wasn't born in a zoo. I was glad that his birth hadn't made headlines—that his picture hadn't been in the paper. I don't know why I was glad but I was.

"Well," I said, turning my attention back to the strange piece of dangling rope he was holding, "what are we gonna do with that?"

Nick turned it over slowly in his hand. He shrugged. Then he looked at me. "Hide it," he said. "Hide it until I think of somethin'."

* * * * *

It didn't take long for Nick to think of something to do with the rope. In fact it was the very next day that he came to me.

"Got an idea," he whispered.

I looked at him and his eyes were twinkling.

He nodded toward a far corner of our cage and I followed him.

"What?" I asked. Excitement made my voice sound funny.

"Sh-h," cautioned Nick and glanced back over his shoulder. We were still safe. Ms. Evangeline was dozing. Mother was busy grooming Mitsy and Father was sitting near the dour Petunia as though to keep her company in her sour mood.

Nick whispered just one word in my ear. "Petunia."

It made my fur stand on end.

I looked at Nick to see if he was serious. He was.

I shifted around nervously. I had the feeling that we were on the road to sure trouble. Yet it was exciting in a way.

"What?" I asked Nick. I couldn't imagine what could be done with the rope that would involve Petunia.

"We'll tie her," said Nick.

Now I was really worried. I looked at Nick and licked my lips nervously.

"You're not gonna hurt her?"

"'Course not," scoffed Nick. "Just have some fun."

I glanced over at Father, sure that he would be reading our minds.

"How?" I asked at last.

"You know how she always has to be first to the food?" Nick hesitated until I responded to his words.

"Yeah."

"Well, the next time—she won't be," said Nick and his eyes twinkled merrily again.

I frowned. I still didn't understand.

Nick seemed to think I was dreadfully slow in comprehension.

"She always naps just before mealtime," he reminded me.

"So?"

"So while she naps, we'll tie her down."

I thought that Nick had taken leave of his senses. "You're crackers," I said to him, giving his shoulder a shove with my fist.

Nick looked angry for a moment. I thought he might punch me. I moved slightly to put a little more distance between us just in case.

But he didn't hit me. He just scowled.

"So you don't want to be in on the fun," he said. He turned from me and started to move away. "Well, that's your loss."

I did want to be in on the fun. I just wasn't sure where Nick's crazy idea would take us.

"Just a minute," I said, following after Nick. I think he knew that I would follow him. He turned and didn't seem at all surprised to see me right behind him.

We sat down again and silently looked at one another. At last Nick spoke. "You in?" he asked me.

I wasn't sure if I was 'in' or not. I hadn't heard Nick's plan yet. But I did know that I sure didn't want to miss any fun.

"What you plannin'?" I asked.

"When she goes to sleep—when they all go to

sleep—we'll just tie her with the rope," he answered. "Then at mealtime when she jumps up to go and eat, she can't."

"How you gonna tie her all up?" I asked, doubt still edging my voice. "The rope isn't long enough to tie a big gorilla."

"Not tie all of her," Nick rejoined, as though I should have known what he meant. "Just one leg."

"One leg?"

"Sure. We'll just wrap the rope around one leg and tie it to—to something."

"What?"

"I dunno. Whatever—whatever it is next to," said Nick.

I thought about that. It might work. The rope would be long enough to reach around one of her legs and still have enough length left to tie it to something else.

I nodded.

"So are you in?"

I thought about that for a minute and then nodded slowly. "I guess so," I said but I still felt some hesitation.

"Good," said Nick.

That one short word sealed our little pact.

*   *   *   *   *

It wasn't long before the missing rope was noticed. That is, it was noticed that it was missing. Georgie stomped all around their enclosure looking for it and asking his family members if they had seen it. Of course none of them had.

I thought about the rope up in the courtyard tree where Nick had tucked it safely away and hoped that he had hidden it well out of sight.

We had to wait until nap time. I wondered if Nick felt as nervous and excited as I did. From his restlessness and his agitation, I judged that he did.

It appeared that the grown-ups were never going to settle down. Father kept playing with his badly misshapen bit of human head-top that he still cherished and wore whenever he could get it to stay on his head.

Mitsy seemed restless and Mother fussed over her in concern. Ms. Evangeline slept, but then she slept a good deal of the time, shifting now and then only to find a more comfortable position.

And Petunia—like always, Petunia fussed and fidgeted and complained and fretted. The bed-nest was too hard—the day was too hot—the birds were noisy—the howlers annoying—the crowd insensitive.

I looked over at Nick. I was quite sure that they were never going to get to sleep.

Nick sent me a silent message. I understood it. I was to pretend that I had already settled down for my nap.

I yawned and wriggled and closed my eyes, hoping that I looked as if I had fallen asleep. I opened one eye enough to catch a glimpse of Nick. He had also stretched out and was feigning sleep. As I watched, one of his eyes opened slightly to survey the adults and their state of slumber. I felt like giggling. But I didn't dare. To laugh would give our little charade away.

It took some time before the heavy breathing of those around me assured me that everyone was really sleeping. All but Nick, that is. At the same time that I stirred, Nick rolled over and away from the others. Without one word to each other, we headed for the exit door to the outer court.

I waited while Nick moved toward the hole in the tree to retrieve the hidden rope. We still didn't speak even though our whispers would not disturb the sleepers from that distance.

Actually, the whole zoo was a symphony of sound. Elephants trumpeted, lions roared, seals barked, and birds called out to one another. Over all of the other sounds, the noise of the howlers out-did everyone. It was a noisy place, the zoo.

Nick picked up the rope and headed for the entrance door, dragging it along behind him. I followed too closely at first. I stepped on the dragging rope, nearly jerking it from Nick's hand and tripping me so that I almost fell on my face. Nick looked up and frowned and I made sure I didn't step on the rope again.

We entered the cage and maneuvered our way among the sleeping bodies. It looked as if it would be easy to get the rope around Petunia's extended leg—but just as Nick went to slip it under her foot, she moved in her sleep and shifted to another position.

I could see the worry enter Nick's eyes. For one awful moment he thought we'd be caught before we'd even had our fun.

We had to wait for what seemed forever before we were sure that Petunia was sleeping soundly again. Then Nick moved cautiously forward. I held my breath.

He reached out to slip the rope around Petunia—and she shifted to her other side. Nick was about to break out into a sweat. He stepped back and held his breath. We had to wait again.

I thought it was never going to work. Just as I was about to give up and suggest that Nick do the same, Nick was able to gently slip the rope around Petunia's ankle and tie an awkward knot to hold it securely in place.

I let out my breath, feeling quite pleased that we had accomplished our mission. Then I looked at Nick. He was holding the other end of the rope in his hand. It wasn't anchored to anything.

"Talk about dumb!" I was thinking. Little good the rope would do tied around Petunia's ankle with nothing to tie it to. Unless Nick planned to sit and hold it. I could hardly see him doing that. The evidence of the mischief would be right in his hands. He could hardly deny that, could he?

Nick was looking around too. There wasn't a thing to fasten to the other end. At least nothing that the short rope would reach.

I expected Nick to give up in disgust and try to get the rope off Petunia's leg before she woke up, so he could get out of there. But he didn't. He looked around. Shifting his weight in frustration, he looked around again—and then he did the dumbest thing. Without hesitation, he leaned over and tied the loose end of the rope to an outstretched arm. That of my father.

I held my breath. What in the world was he thinking of? Surely he knew that he was making one awful mistake. Petunia would awaken and—and—I didn't even want to think about it. I backed away, my eyes big, my thoughts whirling. How could Nick be so—so stupid?

I continued backing up until I backed right out into the courtyard. Before long Nick joined me. He looked pleased with himself. I thought that he had really lost his mind.

"What are you . . .?" I began in a nervous voice but he hushed me and moved away from the door.

"You're crazy, man," I said in a hoarse whisper as we moved away. "Don't you know that Petunia will jump up and it will . . ."

"Exactly," said Nick.

"But she'll . . ."

"I know," said Nick as he rubbed his hands together gleefully.

"But Father hates to be awakened," I hurried on.

"I know," said Nick, his eyes sparkling. "He'll be so angry with Petunia." He looked about to explode with pleasure.

"With *Petunia*?" I hissed, and I gave Nick a slam in the stomach with the back of my hand. "What do you mean, Petunia? He won't think that Petunia tied herself up."

Nick stopped and looked at me. It seemed to be the first that he had considered that possibility.

"What . . ." he began.

"He'll know who did it," I said quickly, "an' it sure won't be Petunia who gets the blame."

Terror filled Nick's eyes. He reached out and grabbed my arm. "Barn, we gotta get that rope off of there," he said frantically.

"*You* gotta get that rope off of there," I corrected him.

He looked back toward our inside home. There wasn't much time. The feeders would be coming with the meal at any time.

"Please, Barn," he pleaded. He looked terribly nervous. "You've gotta help me."

I shook my head.

"It was your idea," I reminded him. "An' your rope—an' you did the tying."

"But . . ." began Nick.

Just then I saw the human with our dinner moving toward our building. I knew that Nick had little time. Maybe no time at all.

"You better get in there," I said to Nick. He swallowed hard and moved toward the door. I followed.

Nick had just approached Petunia when she stirred again. He had to duck back quickly and wait for her to settle.

But it was too late. By the time Nick felt it was safe to move forward again, our dinner was coming in the door.

Petunia was smacking her lips in anticipation before her eyes opened. I was sure that she could smell food miles away—even in her sleep.

As usual, she didn't wait until she was fully awake but rolled over and pushed herself to a sitting position. She was still blinking the sleep from her eyes when she lifted herself and started toward the odor of food.

She had taken only one step when the rope brought her up short and spilled her with a jerk. She toppled forward, screaming at the top of her voice before she even hit the concrete.

The noise alone would have brought my father to his feet, but at the same time that Petunia screamed, the rope gave a mighty jerk on his arm.

With eyes wild, he sprang to his feet, his eyes darting here and there, his hair standing on end in terror and preparation for fight. I saw Nick back off and try to shrivel up into an inconspicuous ball.

Father took one wild look around him and then glanced down quickly at the rope that secured his arm.

I had never seen him so angry. He ripped at the rope with his other hand, giving it such a tug as he tore it from him that he tripped Petunia again, sending her sprawling and screaming and waving her fists in the air.

Father looked first at the end of rope that he held and then toward Petunia who cowered on the concrete floor. It didn't take him long to make the connection. He tossed the end that he held toward the raging Petunia as though, for one ridiculous minute, he thought that she was responsible.

Not only had our whole family been rudely awakened by the uproar, but the animals in the cages next to us had also joined in the commotion. The howlers shrieked in a worse manner than I'd ever heard before. The chimps screamed and hooted and the gibbons bounded back and forth in their cage as though they were being chased by some wild thing. All around, pandemonium had broken out.

I looked at Mother. She looked so frightened that I feared she was going to faint. I wanted to go to her but it hardly seemed the thing to do under the circumstances.

Mitsy was trembling so that her whole body shook. For the first time I began to think of what our impulsive behavior might do to the other members of our family. We had only intended to play a little prank on Petunia. It seemed that our actions were going to be more far-reaching than that. I started to shake. I was scared.

I knew that Nick was scared too. He was backed into a corner. He didn't look cocky now. He looked like a very young gorilla who knew that he was in a great deal of trouble. I wished with all of my heart that I had never listened to his crazy plan.

Chapter Eight

Consequences

It took some time for the commotion to die down. I feared that things might never be normal again but gradually the din lessened.

Actually, it was Father who began to get things under control. As soon as he realized that the family was not being attacked by some strange and mysterious enemy, he began to take stock of what had really happened.

Obviously, it was the rope—only a rope—that had set things off. Father followed the untied end all the way to Petunia's ankle and then, with a disgusted grunt at the whole affair, he loosened her and helped her to her feet.

Petunia was still angry—only this time I knew that she had good reason. Though she appeared not to have been hurt by her fall, she was shaken. It was neither a very smart thing nor a kind thing that we had done.

She brushed at her coat and glared about with angry eyes. Ms. Evangeline left the comfort of her bed and crossed to her. She stroked Petunia with her bony fingers and gently tried to bring her some comfort. I noticed that her eyes did not turn in our direction though I felt sure that she knew we were both cowering in the corner.

Mother turned her attention to Mitsy. Her arm was protectively around the young mother-to-be. She soothed and patted and finally got Mitsy to stop shaking.

As soon as our enclosure began to quiet, the effect spread out to the other cages. Gradually the roar began to lessen. Even the howlers stopped their screaming and went to enjoy their dinner.

The chimps were the last to settle. We were in such close quarters that what affected one family, often affected the other. The final effect came when Father untied the rope and flung it aside where it landed close to the chimp's cage.

Mrs. Chimp began to scream at the top of her lungs, "Snake! Snake!" and had the whole family in an uproar. Mr. Chimp shouted for them all to get back, grabbed his food basin—the only thing that seemed to be available—and ran forward with it upraised, ready to do battle against the wriggling intruder.

Before Mr. Chimp had time to consider his line of defense, Georgie was at his side.

"My rope," he screamed. "That's my rope. It's not a snake. It's my rope."

When it was discovered that the offending piece of rope was lifeless and could do no one harm, Mr. Chimp threw the food dish against the mesh that separated us with such force that the howlers started again.

Father turned from Petunia and looked around our

enclosure. He was beginning to piece things together. I started to shake. I knew that Nick and I were in big trouble.

"You know about this?" Father asked, and his voice sounded like a roar in my ears as his eyes fixed on me.

I wished earnestly that I could deny it. In fact, I was tempted to try. After all I hadn't really been involved—directly. Yet I certainly did know about it. And I never tried to stop it. No. I couldn't say that I wasn't guilty. I had, by my presence at the scene and my approval of Nick's plan, given my assent. I was guilty by association. That's the way Father would see it. A denial would only make my situation worse. I couldn't speak so I just nodded my head.

Nick was close behind me, clinging to me as though I was his only life support.

"And you?" roared Father and I knew that he was speaking to Nick.

"I . . . I . . . Kinda," said Nick in a choking voice.

"Kinda?" raged Father. "Kinda?"

He stood there glaring at us. I felt my wildly beating heart would burst through my chest.

Suddenly Father turned from us. "We'll speak of it later," he said and his voice sounded more natural. He turned to Mother and Mitsy. "Ladies," he said, "Let's have dinner."

I took a deep breath. It seemed that Nick and I might live to see another day after all. Then Father turned his head as he moved away and gave us another angry look. "You'll be last," he said and I

knew his words included both of us.

Nick and I drew back. We were in no position to argue. But I felt my stomach rumble. I hadn't realized how hungry I was until I learned that I would not be allowed to eat yet.

"Didn't I tell . . ." I began in a hoarse whisper, but I didn't get the sentence finished.

"Shut up," Nick said. I said nothing more. Everyone was mad at us and now when the world was against us, it seemed that we couldn't even stick together.

Nick pulled away from me and crossed to another corner. There he sat, all hunched up in a ball. I hadn't realized how small he still was until I saw him there. Why, he didn't look much bigger than me.

I was still mad and scared so I didn't spend much time feeling sorry for Nick. After all, he was the one who had gotten us into the mess.

We had to sit there—just sit right there and watch the adults eat. They took their time about it too, you can be sure of that. I began to fear there would be nothing left by the time it was our turn.

Father dawdled the most. After Petunia was satisfied and had crawled off to lick her wounds, and Mother had moved away with Mitsy, and old Ms. Evangeline was back in her corner napping, Father still sat there. I knew he wasn't hungry. He was just picking through what was left. Nibbling at this or sniffing at that. Now and then he took a bite of something and chewed it like it was a chore rather than a pleasure.

All the time my stomach growled and complained and wanted to be fed. I could hardly stand it.

I looked over at Nick. He was still in a huddle. I saw him look longingly toward the food. He licked his lips in a hungry manner. I suppose his stomach was rumbling just like mine.

At last Father did back away. He never looked toward me. He did not look toward Nick. He just moved off toward Mother and Mitsy and I heard him ask for some grooming. Both ladies turned to him immediately and began the careful process of going over his dark fur, inch by inch.

I wanted to make a dash for the food but I didn't. I still wasn't sure about Nick. He was bigger than I and he seemed quite peevish at the moment.

I let him go first and then I moved forward cautiously.

He didn't really welcome me but he didn't scold either. He gave me one scowling look as though I'd better not say one word if I knew what was good for me and then he started to pick through the food that had been left.

I didn't say anything. I knew better. But I sure did lots of thinking.

We had almost finished our meal when Georgie came to the mesh that divided our enclosures. He pointed a finger at the rope that still lay strung-out on our concrete floor.

"That's my rope," he screamed at us. "That's mine. How'd you get it?"

His screeching brought father to his feet again. He ambled over to where Nick and I were eating what was left of the meal and looked at us with a long, angry stare.

"Is that right?" he asked at last. "Is that his rope?"

I gulped and Nick started to tremble again. I looked at him and he looked at me and then we both looked back at Father.

I nodded.

"How did it get here?" asked Father. His voice told us that we'd better be telling the truth.

I didn't think that I should answer. It was really Nick's doing and I'd be a snitch if I told on him. He managed to get the words out himself. "I . . . I took it," he said.

"You . . . took it?" responded Father. "You . . . took it? Did you have permission to take it?"

Nick trembled.

"Did you?" roared Father.

"No," answered Nick in a tiny voice.

"Then why did you take it?" asked Father in his big, big voice. "Think about it. If it was your rope, would you like someone to take it from you? Would you think they had that right?"

Nick looked up and shook his head as though he didn't have the answer.

"So why did you take it? Why?" demanded Father.

"'Cause," quavered Nick.

"'Cause? 'Cause. That's not too good a reason. 'Cause."

Nick tried to look down but Father's eyes held his.

"I . . . I thought . . . I wanted . . . I . . ." Nick

stumbled to a stop. He shifted nervously and then began again. "To have fun," he managed.

I knew that was the wrong answer. I guess Nick soon realized it too, for Father's glare became more intense.

"Fun?" he nearly exploded. "Fun? So, sending poor Petunia head-over-heels was fun? So, waking me from a sound sleep with the fear of mortal danger, was fun? So, frightening the whole family half to death was fun? Do you know what your fun could have cost your family?"

Nick didn't know what to say. I didn't either, so I held my tongue.

"You stole from your neighbor and you risked the safety of your family—all for fun?" continued Father.

Nick looked up. He was still trembling. "I'm sorry," he managed to say.

"Sorry?" Father said, again repeating Nick's word. "You're sorry. Sorry for what? Sorry you took what didn't belong to you? Sorry you caused distress and alarm? Or sorry that you got yourself in trouble?"

Nick looked down again.

"I'm . . . I'm sorry about . . . about all of it," he managed to say.

For a moment Father continued to glare, then he seemed to soften a bit.

"What's done is done," he said at last. "The results were not as serious as they might have been. But there are always consequences."

Nick nodded.

"First of all, you will take the rope back to the

rightful owner and apologize for the theft. And I never, *never* want to hear of you taking something belonging to another again."

I glanced toward the chimp enclosure. Georgie was standing near the fence. I had the feeling that he was taking great pleasure in seeing us get such a thorough scolding.

Nick nodded.

"Then you will apologize to poor Petunia," continued Father. "You will apologize to each family member." Father stopped and let his words sink in. Then he added, "Except for Barnaby here. Barnaby has some apologizing of his own to be done."

It was my turn to swallow and nod in submission.

"You will both be grounded," resumed Father. "For a week. You will eat last at every meal. And you will not be able to ask for grooming from any family member."

He paused.

"Do I make myself clear?" he asked.

We both nodded. It was clear enough. We were in big trouble.

"Well, then," said Father, "once those apologies are made, I will hear no more of the matter."

He turned and was gone.

I didn't dare look at Nick. And I didn't plan to say, "I told you so," even though I had told him that stolen rope would get us into mischief. Mother said that stolen things always, eventually, cause trouble.

Chapter Nine

Something Unexpected

Nick and I managed to make it through our difficult week of being grounded. Of course Father saw to it that we made all of the necessary apologies for our thoughtless actions. Nick also had to return the rope to Georgie and ask his pardon for what he had done. Georgie was a bit smug about it all. He made a big deal about the rope in the days that followed, always playing with it when Nick and I were around. He probably wanted to remind us that he had the fun of it while we did not.

It was fine with me. I never wanted to see the thing again. Still, there were a lot of enjoyable things that one could do with a piece of rope. Georgie seemed to come up with something new and interesting every other day.

I tried hard to ignore Georgie. I knew that he wanted us to stand around and envy his prized possession. At night he even tied it back at the same spot on our enclosure partition. Perhaps he was hoping that the temptation would be too great and one of us would steal it again.

I never asked Nick any more about the rope. But I knew for sure that I had no desire to get into that kind of trouble again.

Nick seemed to avoid the spot as well and we turned our back on Georgie and his rope and looked around for something else to do.

Before our grounding time had expired, we became friends again. A fellow can stay mad for only so long—especially when you live in the same place as the fellow you are angry at. Mother helped matters between us some, too. She had taught us both that it didn't help to carry a grudge. That just made one even more miserable.

So Nick and I sort of forgot what had happened and started looking for things that would amuse us without getting us into serious trouble.

We spent some time teasing the ants. They were still busy hauling loads back and forth along their little pathway in the corner of the courtyard. That was fun for a while but then it got a little boring.

We pestered a big crow that had taken to sitting in our tree as though he had rightful claim to it. We might have ignored him, had he not started to scold us for every move we made just as though he was the one who owned the place.

There was no way that we could chase him off but our constant badgering kept him squawking and hollering and calling us spoiled, disrespectful, young scamps. Petunia fretted almost as much as he did. She said that he gave her a constant headache. Eventually he left, which was what we wanted in the first place. Afterward, we had to admit that we sort of missed him for it had been fun to harass him.

We spent some time near the glass front of our

enclosure watching the humans who came. We took to mimicking them and making funny faces. They seemed to think it was amusing rather than insulting. That was good, for I'm sure that Father would have stopped us had he thought that we were being disrespectful.

We soon tired of that game as well. Nick and I were both wondering what we could find to entertain us when something interesting happened quite unexpectedly.

Mrs. Sadie Sparrow came flying in with the news. She was breathless and flustered—as she most always was—and we were about to turn our backs and go off to play when her words stopped us.

"Did you know about it?" she asked Mother. "Did the humans tell you?"

Mother looked puzzled.

"Know about what?" asked Mother.

I stopped and sat down. Something out of the ordinary was about to happen.

"Didn't they even ask your permission?" continued Mrs. Sparrow breathlessly.

Mother still frowned.

"Oh, dear," fluttered Mrs. Sparrow. "Oh, dear. Perhaps I've spilled the beans." She cast a nervous glance around the place.

"Well, so be it," she went on, lifting her chin in determination. "Someone should have told you. You should have been notified. You've a right . . ."

"What in the world are you talking about?" interrupted Petunia who had sidled up beside Mother.

"The new one," exclaimed Mrs. Sparrow, wav-

ing a wing. "The new she."

Mother cast a nervous glance around the enclosure. I supposed that she was looking for Father. As head of the family he was the one to look after anything that might affect the whole troop.

But Petunia pushed herself forward and demanded of Mrs. Sparrow rather gruffly, "What in the world are you going on about? What new she? We haven't been told of any new she. Are you sure you know what you're talking about?"

Mrs. Sparrow looked as if her feathers had been ruffled a bit. She gave Petunia a cross look, fluffed up to her plumpest and answered with her head cocked to one side.

"Of course I'm sure," she said haughtily. "I wouldn't be here if I wasn't, now would I?"

Petunia just stared back at her.

Mother turned to me. "Barnaby," she said calmly, "I think you'd better get your father."

I hated to leave. Things were getting interesting and I didn't want to miss a moment of it but I had to obey Mother. I hurried to the courtyard as fast as I could and rushed up to Father who was sitting in his favorite place on the rocks, idly eating a dandelion.

"Father," I said breathlessly. "Mother wants you. There's . . . there's a . . . a new one coming. Mrs. Sparrow said so."

Father frowned at me. I don't think he could make head nor tail of my strange message. But then, I wasn't too sure what it was all about myself.

I ran back in ahead of Father. He seemed to take

his time. I was there, pushing my way into the little circle that had gathered around Mrs. Sparrow's perch, before Father came through the door. Even old Ms. Evangeline had joined the group. She blinked watery eyes and commented quietly, "Now it's nothing to get all upset about. We've had new ones join us before. They have always become a nice part of the family, I've discovered."

Ms. Evangeline gave Mother a pleasant smile. I knew that Mother had been the last one to join this family unit at Roxbury Zoo. Mother and a very young Nick.

The tight little cluster eased back when Father entered. Some of the tension seemed to leave their faces. Father was now in charge. He would see that nothing happened to the family.

Father lifted his eyes to Mrs. Sparrow. For one minute she looked a bit nervous and then she seemed to puff up with importance again.

"What is this all about?" Father asked quietly.

"The . . . the new one," exclaimed Mrs. Sparrow. "I just thought that . . . that you should all know about her."

Father blinked his big eyes.

"Her?" he said. "Who is 'her'?"

"Well, the new one. The one they are bringing here," said Mrs. Sparrow, all aflutter again.

"And who is this new one?" asked Father. "And how do you know she is coming here?"

Mrs. Sparrow, as tiny as she was, dared to give my father a haughty look. "I know," she said rather boastfully, "because I have seen her. And I distinctly heard the keepers talk about keeping her at the zoo hospital for two weeks of quarantine before bringing her here."

"Are you sure?" asked Father.

"Quite!" said Mrs. Sparrow with a flick of her tail. "I wouldn't be here if I wasn't."

Father seemed to be thinking about that. After some time of scratching his chin in silent meditation he turned to the four elders who huddled around him. "Then, in that case," he said, "we will make her feel welcome."

I thought that it was settled.

Father turned back to Mrs. Sparrow. "Thank you," he said simply. "Thanks for bringing us word. It is good to be prepared."

Mrs. Sparrow really puffed up with importance then. She gave Father a nod and then prepared to take off. I figured that she would be busy flitting all around the zoo telling anyone who would listen about how she brought the news to the gorilla family and how the big Silver Back himself had personally thanked her for her consideration.

I turned my eyes back to our little group. Old Ms. Evangeline looked quite content as she blinked her watery eyes and prepared to move slowly back to her bed.

Mother had her arm around Mitsy who had now stopped her shaking. I guess she realized that the newcomer wasn't a threat to her or her unborn baby after all.

Father had turned and picked up the beat-up old human-top from the floor where he had discarded it earlier in the day. He smashed it down on his furry head and blinked out from under the brim. He seemed to feel that the matter of the new family member was properly cared for.

As usual, it was Petunia who decided to make an issue of the matter.

"What's she coming here for?" she exploded. "We have enough mouths to feed. We don't need another member here."

I thought about reminding her that it was the keepers who saw to our provisions—not Petunia—but I held my tongue. I knew that Mother would consider such a statement sauciness on my part. I looked over at Nick and made a face.

"We're already crowded out," Petunia continued. "A body hardly has room to stretch out for a nap. And there's no privacy any more. Not a spot where one can go for a bit of peace and quiet. I don't know why in the world they would even consider crowding another body in here."

I looked around. We had plenty of space. Not only did we have this big, big enclosure but we had all of the room out-of-doors in the huge courtyard as well.

Petunia wasn't finished. "Well, I'll tell you one thing," she continued to fret. "I won't be welcoming her—and you can just count on that." She cast a glance toward Mother and Mitsy. "It isn't enough that we keep over-running the place with new babies who cause all sorts of trouble and confusion," she hissed, "and now this. They've got no right to bring her here. Not a right in the world. I won't be welcoming her. You can just bet on it."

I held my breath and looked anxiously around the little circle. Father had just said, openly and to us all, that the new member was to be welcomed, and here was Petunia daring to defy his order. Wow! I wondered just how Father was going to respond.

He had been sitting there pounding the human-top into yet another weird shape while Petunia made her bold declaration. I wondered if he had even heard her. At first he did not look up. Then slowly, ever so slowly, he raised himself from his sitting position and looked right at Petunia.

"Petunia," he said and his voice was low and calm. "You will be responsible for making our newest member feel at home here. She will be lonely and frightened for a while. I'm sure that you will do all you can to make her feel welcome here." Then he added quite forcefully, "Not just welcome—but wanted."

He walked away, carrying his human-top in his left hand. It squashed into a new shape with every step he took.

I turned to look at Petunia. Her face was flushed. I didn't know if it was anger or embarrassment that was coloring it. But one thing I was sure of. She would not dare to defy Father further. She knew as well as the rest of us did that he would not tolerate it.

Father was King.

* * * * *

"I wonder what she'll be like?" I asked Nick when we were alone later.

He looked up from the hole he was digging in the ground with the sharp end of a stick.

"I dunno," he answered, "but I'll tell you one thing. I sure hope she's not another Petunia."

I thought about that.

Nick went on. "One complainer is more than enough," he continued, and began poking at the ground again.

I kept on thinking.

Then I looked up and said to Nick. "I dunno. Maybe not. Two like Petunia might really make things lively around here. Can't you imagine . . .?"

Nick stopped poking with his stick. His eyes lit up. I knew that he was envisioning what it would be like with two people like Petunia continually rubbing one another the wrong way. Boy, could that make for some interesting moments.

"Hey," he said. "Wouldn't that be a hoot?"

"Poor Father," was my only comment. He, as head of the family, would have a tough job sorting things out and trying to keep the peace.

Nick went back to digging.

"Well, that's not likely," he said, and he sounded quite disappointed. "I don't suppose there are two like Petunia in the whole wide world."

I guessed he was probably right. I felt a bit disappointed too.

We sat quietly for a few minutes, Nick digging, me watching. At last I broke the silence.

"What you doin'?" I asked him.

"Diggin'," he replied.

"Diggin' what?"

"A hole."

I could see that.

"What for?" I asked next.

Nick just shrugged his shoulders. "To see where it goes," he replied.

I looked at him and frowned. "It don't go nowhere," I told him.

He looked up at me. "Does too," he argued. "Look. It already goes all the way down there." He pointed at the little hole he had dug in the soft ground. "And it's gonna go even farther by the time I'm done," he continued. "Just wait and see if it don't."

I looked at him. It made no sense to me. None at all. I shrugged and moved away, shaking my head.

I wondered what he thought he was accomplishing. He could dig all he wanted with his little stick. I knew that hole was going nowhere.

Chapter Ten

The New One

"Do you think she'll come today?" I asked Mother anxiously as we stretched to get the kinks from our muscles after our night's sleep. It seemed to me that the days had been passing at a snail's pace since Mrs. Sparrow had brought us the news. I was beginning to doubt that she had her facts straight.

Mother just yawned and smacked her lips. She reached out a hand and rubbed the top of my head.

"Do you?" I insisted.

Mother sat up and gathered me close for a minute. She still held me whenever I could be still enough to be held.

"Do you?" I repeated.

Mother shook her head. "I've no idea," she said.

"But it's already been . . . been . . . forever," I said with some indignation. "Maybe Mrs. Sparrow didn't . . . wasn't . . ."

"Oh, she was right about it," said Mother. "Max Mouse brought the same report."

"Then why hasn't she . . .?"

"I don't know," interrupted Mother. "Sometimes they need to stay in quarantine a bit longer than usual."

"Why do they stay in . . . in quarantine, anyway?" I asked.

"Quarantine?" Mother smacked and yawned again. "The keepers. That's the way the human keepers check to be sure the new animals don't bring any sickness to the rest of us."

"Sickness?" The very word brought me fear.

Mother nodded.

"Can she bring sickness?" I asked, more worried than impatient now.

Mother shook her head. "I don't suppose," she said distractedly. "She's been in quarantine. They'll check. They'll watch."

Mother playfully began to tussle with me. I knew that she was trying to take my mind off the coming of the new member.

It was always that way. The adults didn't talk about her. They seemed to be pretending that it wasn't going to happen. That it really wouldn't make any difference to our family unit. But there was tension in the air. I could feel it. Nick had remarked about it too. Sometimes I felt that things were just going to explode.

Petunia didn't help matters any. Oh, she didn't talk about the new member. She didn't dare because she couldn't say anything positive and she didn't dare complain about it any more. Not since Father had given her the responsibility to make the new member welcome.

So, because Petunia couldn't talk about the new gorilla who was coming to live with us, she talked about everything else. If she had been annoying before, she was terrible now. She fussed and grumped and complained until I thought that she would surely drive us all crazy. Nick and I sort of swung back and forth. Some days we tested and tormented her just for the fun of hearing her whine and on other days we tired of her constant complaining and stayed as far away from her as we could get.

I never heard Father say one word about the new-comer but I noticed that he was a bit edgy as well. He wasn't quite as patient with me when I wanted to play around him. Nick and I both withdrew a bit, waiting for the new-arrival day to come so the family could get back to normal again.

It seemed to me that the time would never come. I began to get a little edgy myself. I wished that Mrs. Sparrow had just kept her news to herself.

* * * * *

No sooner had I dismissed my thought of Mrs. Sparrow than she came soaring into our room. She was totally aflutter and out of breath. We all looked up, knowing she was convinced that she was the bearer of some important news.

"She's coming! She's coming!" she chirped ex-citedly.

Father shifted his weight on his broad bottom. He smacked his lips and blinked his eyes.

"You told us," he reminded Mrs. Sparrow.

"No! I mean now," she hurried on. "They are on their way. I mean—right now. She's already in the transport pen."

I could feel a ripple pass around the little circle. No one said a word but bodies shifted uncomfortably and eyes blinked and hands lifted and then fell back to laps.

She was coming. Finally. What would happen now? What would she be like? Would she fit in well with our troop? Would she be a trouble-maker? Another complainer? Old and arthritic?

A stirring in the corner distracted us. Old Ms. Evangeline was raising herself slowly from her bed. She sat for a minute and ran her fingers over her coat as though making sure that she looked her best. Then she came slowly forward and sat down right beside Father.

"How nice to finally get to meet her," she said, and she looked like she really meant the words.

Father nodded. He, too, ran a hand over his well-groomed body. Then he shifted himself to all fours and ambled off toward the farthest corner of our enclosure. From the darkness he lifted something and carried it back to where he sat down in the family circle again.

Taking the object in both his hands he lifted it and smacked it down hard on the top of his head. It was the battered, misshapen human-top that he had come to treasure. It was hardly recognizable any more. Father had thumped and twisted, fingered and pommelled it so much that one could barely figure out what it was supposed to be.

But Father seemed to feel better with the favored item placed haphazardly on his furry brow.

We didn't need to wait long. Mrs. Sparrow was

still there busily and nervously fluttering about when we heard the commotion of someone coming to the strange little door at one end of our enclosure.

They were talking human-talk so I didn't understand all their words. But they did have an unfamiliar big box. It wasn't solid but had windows and bars at the sides and I knew that something was moving around inside even though I couldn't get a good look.

I held my breath. I could hardly wait to see who she was.

It seemed to take forever. The humans fiddled and dawdled and took more time than it should have taken to just dump off one more gorilla and then move on. I couldn't understand what caused the delay.

While this was going on, the family just sat. Sat right there watching and waiting—not saying one word—just watching and waiting.

I thought I was going to burst. The suspense and the long time of sitting—just sitting as still as a rock—made all of my muscles and nerves tighten up and want to explode.

But, of course, I didn't explode. I didn't dare. The tension in the room was too acute.

Quite suddenly, all of the humans, all of the noise, all of the clutter of box and bars, were gone. And there, just inside the strange little door, sitting all alone and looking scared and uncertain, was the new member of our family. I heard myself take a big breath. I couldn't believe what my eyes were seeing.

She was so tiny. Why, she was even smaller than Nick. She just sat there, blinking big eyes and looking too frightened to move.

Father approached her first. He moved slowly. I was sure he was thinking that his huge size would frighten her even more. He stopped before he reached her and sat down.

For a few moments they just looked at one another and then Father said, "Hello."

"Hello," she answered and her voice was so soft that I could hardly hear her.

"I'm Sam," said Father. "Folks call me Big Sam, but just Sam is fine."

She nodded. She still looked afraid to move.

"And your name?" prompted Father.

"Twinkie," she answered. "Just—Twinkie."

Father nodded. He pushed up onto his hands and feet and nodded toward the rest of us who sat in a little cluster observing our new mate.

"Come meet the rest of the family, Twinkie," Father offered.

She looked hesitant but followed him. She was so little. So shy. I looked over at Mother and caught the look in her eye. I could see that she was thinking of doing some more mothering.

Father stopped before us and sat back down.

"This is Ms. Evangeline," he said with a nod toward her.

Ms. Evangeline looked at the little gorilla and nodded her head. Her eyes looked teary but I wasn't sure if it was because she was feeling sentimental or if they were just giving her trouble again.

Twinkie nodded politely.

Ms. Evangeline reached out one of her bony hands and patted Twinkie on the arm. She didn't say anything but I think that Twinkie understood.

"And this is Rosie," continued Father, indicating my mother.

Again Twinkie gave a nod of acknowledgement. I knew that it was hard for Mother to keep from giving the little thing a warm hug. She restrained the impulse, but I was sure there would be many warm hugs in the days ahead.

"And Mitsy," said Father, nodding toward Mitsy who was getting more round and uncomfortable with each passing day.

I expected Father to introduce Petunia next, but he didn't. He turned to Nick and me.

"This is Nick," he said with a nod. For once Nick was totally still and totally silent. He did not even blink. He just looked and looked at young Twinkie.

"And Barnaby," resumed Father.

With the mention of my name, I turned my attention from Nick back to Father. I gave the proper response to the introduction and quickly looked back at Nick again. He was still staring.

Then Father turned to Petunia. "And this is Petunia," he said and there was a certain firmness in his voice. "She is going to make you feel at home with us. She has been waiting for your arrival. I'm sure you are tired after your journey and would like to freshen up. Petunia will be happy to do some grooming."

I watched Petunia. I could see her eyes flash, then

quickly fade. I knew that she wasn't too thrilled with her assignment. In her thinking, the new young member should be grooming her.

But she didn't argue. She nodded toward Twinkie without one word and led the way to a private spot where the required grooming could take place in an unhurried fashion.

I still hadn't moved. Nor had I spoken. We had looked forward to this event for days and now that it had arrived, it really seemed of very little import. I was a bit disappointed. I turned to Nick, about to shrug off the event and ask him what all of the fuss had been about anyway. We had been expecting an adult member. Maybe bossy or critical, or sweet and overbearing, or old and needing care, and here all we got was this little thing. She was just a kid.

"C'mon," I said over my shoulder to Nick. "Let's go find somethin' to do."

There was no movement beside me. I turned to look at Nick. He still just sat there staring—open-mouthed. I couldn't figure out what was wrong with him.

"C'mon," I said again. "This is boring."

"Wow!" said Nick, not even looking at me. "Wow! She's cute."

"What you talkin' about?" I asked him, stopping dead in my tracks.

Nick acted like he didn't hear my question.

"I thought they said it was a missus," murmured Nick in a funny voice.

"They didn't say a missus," I corrected him. "Just a she."

"She's cute," Nick said again.

I looked over at the young gorilla. I supposed she was cute. Kinda. But I sure didn't see what that had to do with us.

"Let's go," I said again. This time Nick followed but he really didn't seem to be concentrating on the game of tag that we played. I beat him easily every time.

Chapter Eleven

Getting Acquainted

Things didn't improve much in the days that followed. Nick, who had been my very best friend and my only real playmate, now seemed to be in some sort of stupor. Even when I did talk him into playing a game with me, his mind wasn't on it. He was always looking off toward Twinkie to see if she was watching. He did some pretty silly things to get her attention, too—like trying to turn a somersault in the air while jumping off Father's favorite sitting-rock, or spinning the tire over his head with one hand. It thumped down and hit him on the ear and he had a hard time to keep from howling.

Even that didn't stop him. Oh, no. He still kept showing off. I couldn't figure out what had happened to him.

I complained to Mother about it. She just patted my head and ruffled my fur and then began her own little game with me. Mother could be very playful at times.

I had no quarrel with the new Twinkie. I mean, she wasn't mean or pushy or anything like that. In fact, she could be quite fun at times. The older family members all seemed to like her just fine. She did her share of the family chores and was always more than willing to groom. Petunia took advantage of the fact, of course, and would have monopolized Twinkie's time had not Father made a new rule.

It wasn't Twinkie so much—it was Nick. He had changed so much that he wasn't fun any more. At least, no fun for me. I guess Twinkie thought that he was fun. At least they were together an awful lot. I got pretty fed up with it.

Mother accused me of pouting. Of course I denied that. I wasn't pouting. I mean, I had a good reason to be feeling angry inside. My best friend had just deserted me for another playmate. And she wasn't even as good at tag or hide-and-seek as I was.

One day I was feeling particularly mixed-up inside. Nick was showing off again. He wasn't paying any attention to me. I sat there looking glumly out at the crowd that shifted and interchanged on the other side of the big glass wall. I didn't even find them interesting. In the cage to our left, the howlers jumped and swung, putting on quite a show. Even that didn't draw my interest. I was bored—bored—bored. And mad—mad—mad too, I guess.

I picked up a little twig that someone had brought in from outside and began to thump at the concrete floor with it. Life was a mess. It just wasn't fun any more. Nobody paid any attention to me. I might as well be—be on the moon—or on a deserted island—or in the middle of a jungle—or something.

"Hi," said a voice behind me.

I jumped.

I hadn't been expecting anyone to speak to me. I turned and looked.

"Hi," he said again. It was Georgie. He was right behind me on the other side of our dividing partition.

I squirmed my body around without getting up and gave him a nod. "Hi," I answered, but I knew I didn't sound too enthused.

"Whatcha doin'?" he asked.

"Just—just—thumpin'," I answered.

"I know a new trick with my rope," said Georgie. "Wanna see?"

I really wasn't interested in Georgie's rope tricks but I nodded anyway. I looked at the rope. Georgie had nearly worn it out since the time that Nick had borrowed it and got us into so much trouble.

The trick wasn't that great. He just sort of swung the thing around and then jumped over the dragging end of it. I guess I didn't respond with too much enthusiasm.

"You and Nick have a fight?" he asked with a frankness that surprised me.

"Naw," I said quickly. "We didn't fight."

He sort of squatted on the other side of the partition and looked through the mesh at me.

"What's the matter with him?" he asked me.

I glanced over at Nick. He was goofing around with one of the food basins. Just as I looked up I saw him overturn it, reach up and place it on top of his head. The very same old trick that Georgie had used for so many years to entertain the crowd, and at which Nick had scoffed.

Twinkie looked delighted and Nick puffed up his chest a bit.

"He sick?" prompted Georgie.

I turned to look at Nick. I hadn't even considered that possibility. "Naw," I said, quite sure that wasn't the problem. Something would have been said if Nick were sick.

"My ma says he has a crush," went on Georgie.

"A crush?" I didn't know what he was talking about.

"What's a crush?" I asked Georgie, frowning at the strange new word.

"I dunno," said Georgie with a shrug of his shoulders, "but that's what my ma says."

I looked back at Nick. Something surely was wrong with him but I couldn't figure out what it was.

* * * * *

From then on I spent a good deal of time at the fence with Georgie. There wasn't much that we could do for games with the big dividing mesh between us, but at least he was someone to talk to. He wasn't really a bad sort. In fact, I figured that we could have had fun together if we'd been given a chance.

The crowds of humans came and went. There were still those who stopped and pointed and called out excitedly, "Look, there's Roxie." It always made my day but it didn't happen quite as often anymore. I kind of missed it. After all, I was still the only gorilla in the family who'd had his picture on the front page of the paper.

Even the calls failed to make me feel good for
long. Nothing really made me feel good. Deep down,
I was smart enough to know that my misery wasn't
all Nick's doing. Maybe I *was* pouting just a little.
When Nick stopped his showing-off for Twinkie and
came to see if I'd like to play tag or wrestle or tease
the ants, I never felt like doing it. Maybe I wanted
to show Nick that I didn't need him any more than
he needed me.

I don't quite know why I acted that way. It made
me feel sort of important to turn Nick down, but
as soon as he gave up and walked away I felt sad
inside. I often wanted to call him back and say I'd
changed my mind. But I never did. I just sat and
sulked. There wasn't much else to do when one was
all alone.

The days were really quite boring. There may
have been interesting things going on somewhere.
Mother seemed to think that the daily gossip round
that Mrs. Sparrow made brought many things to think
and talk about. She and Mitsy were quite excited
as they shared about the leak in the walrus tank or
the dispute between the polar bear and the grizzly.
Or the new twins born to Mrs. White-Tail Deer.

I didn't pay much attention to the gossip. I was
still a bit put out with Mrs. Sparrow. If she hadn't
brought us the news about the new family member,
then maybe Twinkie would not have come to live
with us. And if Twinkie had not come, maybe Nick
would still be my best friend. And if Nick were my
best friend and paying attention to me instead of this

new girl, then maybe I wouldn't be feeling so lonely and bored.

It was all a terrible mix-up as far as I was concerned. And it might not have happened if only busybody Mrs. Sparrow had just minded her own business.

I wished with all of my heart that things could go back to the way they used to be.

Then I heard Mother and Mitsy talking.

I was sitting there just scratching and staring, not doing anything or even thinking very much, when I heard a voice right beside me. I hadn't realized that they had moved so close to me and were busy grooming one another.

". . . sure has changed," the voice said. I knew that it was Mother speaking. My ears perked up. I figured that she was talking about Nick and maybe she'd tell some secret that I would be interested in.

"My, yes," said Mitsy sounding a bit breathless and excited. "I never would have believed that someone could change so much."

Must be Nick, all right, I said to myself.

"I can't get over how peaceful and quiet it is in the family now," continued Mitsy.

"Isn't it wonderful?" That was Mother again. "My, I would hate to go back to how things used to be."

Mitsy sighed. "Oh, me too," she said. "Everything is so—so serene now. Why I even heard the chimps talking about it yesterday."

There was silence for a few minutes. So even the chimps had noticed the difference in Nick. Well, I knew Georgie had. And his mother had too. She had

said he was 'crushed' or something like that. I still
hadn't found out what the word meant.

"I'm so glad she came," sighed Mitsy.

She? I knew that the only she who had come
was Twinkie.

"It has changed our lives," stated Mother. "We
should all be deeply thankful for the peace she has
brought us."

There, they said it again. They kept talking about
the new peace that we were all experiencing. I knew
that Nick had been a bit mischievous. He had even
gotten a bit carried away at times but surely he
hadn't been that bad. Many times I had heard Mother
say that he was just being a kid. That he would grow
up in due time. That he hadn't really done anything
that outrageous. Now they were talking as if he had
disrupted the whole family and Twinkie had mysteriously settled him into a respectable family member.

"What do you think—I mean—why do you think
it's made such a difference?" asked Mitsy.

Mother seemed to be considering her answer.
When she spoke, her voice was heavy with emo-
tion. "Love," she said. "I think that she has been—
well—needing to be needed for a long time. When
Twinkie came and she was assigned to care for her,
what she had expected to be a burden, she found
to be a privilege. I . . . I hoped the minute I saw
the young thing that it would happen that way. Why,
I think that Petunia sees her as . . . as her own
youngster. She took over her care because it was
an order, and when Twinkie responded so easily and

quickly—well, Petunia just found what she needed. Someone to love."

Wait a minute, I thought, my head coming up quickly. I thought you were speaking of Nick.

"Poor Petunia," Mitsy said in that little, whispery voice. "I guess none of us understood her very well."

Mother seemed to agree. Then she added softly, "But it is so nice not to have her constantly angry and complaining all the time now. My, we should all be deeply thankful that Twinkie came to us when she did."

"Yes," sighed Mitsy. "She is such a sweet little thing."

I couldn't believe what I was hearing. I didn't want to believe what I was hearing. I left them and went over and sat down against the far wall by myself.

From where I was, I could see Petunia and Twinkie. Petunia was sitting with one arm protectively around the youngster. I hadn't thought of it before but it was true. Petunia had begun to treat Twinkie just like she was her own.

And Twinkie had responded. She was bright and cheerful and quick to obey. All of the adults seemed to love her, especially Petunia who was quite possessive of Twinkie and was quick to let the rest of the family know that the youngster was her charge.

I tried to think back and remember. When was the last time that I had heard Petunia rant and rage about something? When had she last complained about the food? The bed? The noise from next door? It was true. I just hadn't thought about it, but it was

true. Petunia had changed. Tremendously. And it was due to Twinkie. None of the adults wanted to return to the way things were before Twinkie came.

I slumped down against the wall. Guess it wouldn't do much good for me to campaign to get Twinkie sent back to wherever she'd come from. Nick was too—crushed or something—and Petunia pampered and fussed over Twinkie. The rest of the adults thought that she had changed their world for the better. I was the only one who wished she hadn't come. The only one who had somehow been lost in all of the changes. Everyone had practically forgotten that I existed and there didn't seem to be a thing that I could do about it.

It didn't seem fair. Mother often said that life isn't always fair. She said sometimes things happen to us that we don't like, and we just have to adjust.

But then Mother was always saying things like that. She just didn't understand about some things.

I was glad for one thing. I was still the only one who had made the front pages. I was still the one that people came to see. They pointed and shouted and seemed excited to see me. "There he is! There's Roxie," they would say and I'd move closer to the big glass window so they could get a better look.

Then I always turned and looked slyly around for Nick and Twinkie. I earnestly hoped that they had noticed.

I was still the most important gorilla at the zoo.

Chapter Twelve

Another Change

I awoke with a start. The whole family seemed to be stirring. I opened one eye to see what was going on. It seemed that morning had come much too soon.

Then I realized that it wasn't morning yet. I rolled over on my side and wrapped myself up in my arms again.

But there was still movement about me. I heard whispers too. Something strange was going on.

"It's time," I heard Mother say to Father and he sat bolt upright blinking away the sleepiness from his eyes.

Mother moved away from the group, her arm around Mitsy. They should be lying back down to sleep, I thought. It wasn't time to get up yet.

"Where they goin'?" I asked Father sleepily, rubbing my eyes with the hairy back of my hand.

"She'll be back," he answered me. "She's just going to get Mitsy settled."

Settled? That sounded strange. Mitsy had been settled. Snuggled right down with the rest of us.

I tried to go back to sleep but I couldn't. I noticed that Father kept shifting and stirring as well.

But he was right. It wasn't long until Mother was back, but she didn't have Mitsy with her.

"Where's Mitsy?" I asked Mother in a hoarse whisper.

"It's time," said Mother.

"Time?"

"For the new baby," Mother went on. "She needs her privacy now."

"Privacy?"

"To be alone." Mother nodded toward the corner where Mitsy was busily preparing her own private place. Nesting.

Now I began to understand. That was where Mother had taken Mitsy. That was where the new baby was to be born.

We all lay back down and tried to go back to sleep but there was shifting and whispering and constant disruption. Father finally gave up altogether and left the group to go out into the courtyard under the stars.

Mother got up and moved closer to the corner where Mitsy had now settled. I could tell by the way Mother kept turning her head that she was listening carefully to what was going on.

I could have slept had I been given the opportunity. I was still tired. Nick was still sleeping soundly. I could hear his even breathing. But he was a little farther from all of the confusion and commotion than I had been. I wanted to go over and lay down beside him but, at the same time, I didn't want to either. So I just stayed where I was and tossed and turned right along with Petunia and

Twinkie.

I thought morning would never come. But it did. Mother was still sitting near the corner, keeping vigil. Father was still pacing back and forth out in the courtyard. Now and then I could hear him grunt or thump his human-top around. It seemed to me that it was taking an awfully long time for that new baby to make its appearance. Maybe someone had made a mistake. Maybe there wasn't going to be a new baby, after all.

I went out into the courtyard to see what kind of day it was going to be. The sun was already warming up the ground and the rock where Father sat. It was going to be another hot day. I liked the heat. It was so nice to stretch out on the grass and feel the warm fingers of the sun rub all of the kinks from one's back.

I spoke to Father but he didn't give me much of an answer. I think his mind was on something else for he just grunted and thumped at his human-top again.

I hadn't been in the courtyard very long when Twinkie came bursting out, her bright little eyes shining.

"It's come," she squealed to Father. "It's come. Rosie says to come in and see."

Father turned. His eyes began to sparkle. He lifted the human-top from his shaggy brow and thumped it one last good thump. Then he dropped down on all fours and quickly followed Twinkie back into our enclosure.

I was right behind him. But I was stopped before I got far.

"Sh-h-h," said Petunia hoarsely. "Sh-h-h."

I took a few more tentative steps.

"Sh-h," said Mother moving noiselessly toward me. "Sh-h."

"Why . . .?" I began but Mother moved closer to me and whispered. "They need to rest. Both of them."

She nodded her head toward the corner nest where Mitsy sat upright cradling something in her arms. Father was moving toward her.

"Can I see?" I asked. I was curious about this new little one.

"Later," said Mother. "Later. They need to rest now."

"But Father . . ." I began.

"He won't stay long," said Mother. "He just wants a peek at Mitsy's new daughter."

"Daughter? You mean it's a girl?"

Mother nodded. She looked very pleased. I had hoped that the new baby might be another boy.

We had barely finished our whispered conversation when there was a commotion outside our enclosure. A new sign was being posted.

We all gathered in a huddle and exchanged glances. What were they saying now?

Mother looked around to see if any of the mouse family might be around helping themselves to leftovers. Then she looked upward to see if any of the sparrows were perching above us. There didn't seem to be a soul around.

I saw her look of disappointment. We were all

terribly curious about the sign.

Just then there was a stirring in the corner. One of the young mice had just come in. Mother called to him immediately. "Can you read?" she asked him.

He nodded. "Some," he said.

"Will you check the sign, please?" asked Mother.

With a flick of his tail he was gone. I knew that he felt important for being asked to do such a task. It seemed to take him an unusually long time. When he came back, he was all out of breath. "It says," he said, puffing with each word, "It says: *Roxbury's latest—something. Roxie, our first baby—something. Then—something else about Number One.*"

That's what the sign had said about me. Were they saying the same thing about this new baby? How could they? That was me. I was Roxie. I was the first baby born at Roxbury Zoo.

I felt anger raise my neck hair. How could they use my sign for another baby?

"No, no," Mother was saying to the young mouse. "The other sign. The new one—right there."

The mouse looked embarrassed but he quickly regained his composure. "Why didn't you say you meant the new one?" he asked a bit cockily.

"I'm so sorry," said Mother. "I should have thought."

Off he went again. We all stood in our little cluster waiting breathlessly for his return.

He slid to a stop and brushed quickly at his whiskers. "It says," he began, "in big letters, *It's a girl.* Then in little letters it says—*something else*—I don't know all the words. But it says *zoo* and it says

newest and it says *Number One*. That's all I know."

I know that Mother was disappointed not to have the whole message but she thanked the little mouse politely and told him he'd done a wonderful job. He puffed up his small chest, tweaked his whiskers again, and was gone as quickly and mysteriously as he had come. I guessed he was off to tell his family of his new-found importance as sign-reader to the gorillas.

Later I was given my first peek of the new cousin. Boy, was she a little thing. I was amazed at her size. Mother said she weighed about five pounds. That wasn't very big when one remembered that Father weighed close to four hundred.

She didn't do much of anything. Just lay there close against Mitsy who held on to her like she'd never let her go. The baby didn't even open her eyes. I didn't think that she was going to be much of a playmate. In fact, I didn't suppose that she was going to be much good for anything.

The whole family seemed awfully taken with her. She was all that they talked about. All that they thought about. Even old Ms. Evangeline had to hobble over to get a good look at her and declared her to be 'a precious little sweetie.' Everyone fussed over her. Even Father.

It didn't bother me too much. After all she really wouldn't affect my life to any degree. I dismissed her as rather unimportant and went out to see Georgie. He'd been boasting that he had a new trick and he was going to have Minx help him with it. It was a 'two-chimp trick' he told me and I was looking forward to what he had dreamed up now.

* * * * *

Mitsy didn't join the family much for a few days and, when she did, she had that new little bundle of arms, legs and fur, tucked in close to her. Already the little thing had fistfuls of Mitsy's fur clutched tightly in balled-up fingers. She wasn't very big but she could sure hold on.

Mitsy didn't seem to mind the family pressing in about her, sneaking peeks at the baby, stroking her little head, or counting her little fingers. But she didn't seem to like the crowd of humans who gathered close to the glass. When the big doors opened and the noisy, milling crowd swept in, Mitsy moved farther into the darkness of her corner, holding her baby close in protective arms until one could hardly see that she had a baby there at all.

I hadn't thought much more of the sign. The one that said, *It's a girl.* It didn't seem that important to me. However, Mother had not forgotten it. The very next time that Mrs. Sparrow came fluttering in, Mother asked her if she'd mind just taking a peek to see what it said. Of course Mrs. Sparrow didn't mind. She loved to be the bearer of news. Any news.

"It says," she came back saying, *"It's a girl. Roxbury Zoo's newest gorilla baby. She's tiny and cute and Number One. Her name is Roxanne."*

She was breathless by the time she had relayed the long message. Tipping her head and puffing her feathers, she looked quite proud of herself.

"Thank you," said Mother. "Thank you so much."

But I was miffed. Number One? What did they mean, Number One? I was the one who'd had my picture in the paper. I was the zoo's first baby gorilla. I was the important one. Had someone forgotten? It was me that the crowds came to see. It was me that they pointed at and called out, "There he is. There's little Roxie. Look at him. Isn't he cute?"

Surely someone, somewhere had made a big mistake. I hoped that they would get it corrected soon, before it caused some confusion.

Chapter Thirteen

The Lesson

Mother knew that I was upset by the news Mrs. Sparrow had brought, but I don't think she really understood how much it bothered me.

"But I'm Number One," I insisted. She gently ran her hand over my head. "Yes, Barnaby. You were number one. That will never change. Once is all it happens. You will always have been the first baby gorilla born at Roxbury Zoo. Even when you are old and silver-backed—no matter how many babies come after you—you will still be the first—always."

I suppose Mother thought that her words would bring me comfort. And maybe they did—a little bit. But I was still upset that the sign had it all wrong. Somebody needed to get out there and change that sign to what it should be. I was Number One—and Mother said that I always would be.

It didn't help much that everyone in the family was fussing over the new baby girl. The sign said that her name was Roxanne but Mitsy paid no mind to that and named her Rosanna after my mother. I know that pleased Mother and she often talked about little Rosie just as if she partly belonged to her. I didn't like that either.

Everyone was paying attention to the new baby.
Everyone. I still couldn't see what made her so special. She didn't do a thing but cling to her mother.

In my frustration, I found half of a cantaloupe
that had been left from breakfast, and moved over
to sit where the crowd could see me a little better.
I guess I needed to hear them shout excitedly, "There
he is. There's Roxie. He's Number One."

I found a nice spot to sit and started to work on
my snack, coaxing the sweet, fleshy fruit away from
the rind with my teeth and tongue. I had only taken
a few bites when there was a stirring on the other
side of the near-by partition.

"Hi."

It was Jenny Lou.

I brightened. I always liked to talk with Jenny
Lou. She liked me.

"Hi," I answered and pivoted around so that I
could see her better. Now my back was partly to
the crowd at the window. I was sorry about that but
it couldn't be helped.

"I haven't seen you for a while," said Jenny Lou.
"At least not to speak to. I've seen you across your
enclosure. Guess things have been pretty busy at your
house."

I nodded. I hadn't been busy and wasn't quite sure
what she was talking about but I pretended to understand.

"That's the way it always is with a new baby,"
continued Jenny Lou.

Oh, the new baby, I thought, and glanced over
to where Mitsy sat in the half-shadows. Petunia was

doing some grooming on Mitsy's coat, Mother was hovering nearby, and Twinkie was looking like she was ready to dash off on an errand—any errand— should someone give the command. Yes, a new baby was a lot of work alright. I wouldn't deny that.

I nodded again.

"I sure wish I could see her," she sighed.

I looked up from my cantaloupe.

"She don't amount to much," I said frankly.

"Is she . . .?"

Before she could finish her question, I had my answer ready. "She's not much bigger than Father's hand," I said, "an' she don't talk or walk or nothin'."

Jenny Lou almost swooned. "Oh-h-h," she said. "She must be so sweet."

I shook my head. I hadn't noticed anything sweet about the new baby.

"Oh, I'd love to see her. Do you think that Ms. Mitsy would bring her to the partition?"

I shrugged. "I dunno," I said. "She still doesn't like the crowds."

Jenny Lou looked out at the people pressing against the front glass. "I don't blame her," she said. "If I had a new baby, I'd keep her back in the shadows too."

I thought about that. "Well, I think that Mitsy is wise to keep this one there," I said sourly. "She isn't anything but arms and legs and a pinched-up face."

"Oh-h-h," said Jenny Lou. "She must be so cute. I'd just love to see her."

I liked Jenny Lou even though I couldn't understand her interest in that new baby. But then, maybe

Jenny Lou just liked babies. She was always caring for the younger ones in her own family.

"I'll ask her," I said, nodding my head toward Mitsy. "I'll ask her. After the crowd is gone and the doors are shut. Maybe she won't mind then."

"Oh, thank you. Thank you, Barnaby," said Jenny Lou and she was so pleased about it that I felt pretty good for a few minutes. Jenny Lou went skipping off to share her good news with the other chimps and I went back to nibbling on my cantaloupe.

The crowd was getting bigger and bigger. Folks were studying the signs and leaning forward to look into our enclosure and talking their strange talk in excited voices. I began to puff out my chest. It was nice to be so popular. So sought out and known by so many.

"Look. There. See? Back in the shadows. I think I see her. Look. Her mother is holding her. It's her. I'm sure. It's the new baby. Roxanne. There she is. Right there. Roxanne."

I couldn't believe my ears. I understood the name and the excitement and the pointing fingers. Not one finger was pointing my direction. Not one voice was calling out my name. It was all the same. "Roxanne. Roxanne." It was that crazy, mistaken sign that had done it. The humans read it and believed that the new baby, Roxanne, was Number One.

I couldn't take it. I threw what was left of my cantaloupe at the glass with all my strength. It went *splat* and made an awful gooey mess on the window before the rind went sliding down the side and plunked into the concrete gutter below. I didn't stop to look. Angrily, I left the enclosure. I had to get out. I had to get away. I had to put some space between myself and that new baby.

I went out to the courtyard. No one else was there. They were all inside fussing over that new little "bundle."

I stomped around for a while, shuffling my feet angrily and swatting at anything that got in my way. It wasn't fair. It just wasn't fair. Why should things happen that changed everything? I had been so special to everyone in the family, and now—now they didn't seem to even notice me any more. It wasn't fair.

I walked and grumbled and managed to cool down a little bit but I was still really upset. Mrs. Sparrow flew over and called to me cheerily but I didn't even look up. Mother would have been shocked at my lack of manners. But I didn't care. I didn't care about anything. Why should I? No one cared about me any more.

I walked and fumed until I was almost tuckered out. Having a miff can really be exhausting. At last I climbed up on Father's big rock and tried to think.

I couldn't. I was still too upset. My brain just didn't seem to work right. Every time that I began to make some sense of it all, I got mad all over again and then I forgot all of the good reasoning that I had just done.

I finally gave up trying to figure it out and went over to tease the ants. At least that was something to do.

I found a small stick and plopped myself down

on the ground beside the ant pathway. Three big ants were marching in a row, each with something tightly clutched in its small ant-mouth. I stuck the stick in front of them.

For a moment they seemed uncertain as to what to do. They scurried around this way and that but they didn't drop their loads. Oh, no. They just hung on as if their lives depended upon it.

At last they seemed to get themselves sorted out and away they went again. Single file. Right around the end of my stick. I moved it over. They were halted again. Then I did something that I had never done before. I took the stick and I gave it a whish. All three ants went flying through the air. They landed nearby, totally confused and agitated. They scurried around and around as though trying to remember which way they had been heading. But they still had their loads firmly in their mouths.

And then the strangest thing happened. I don't really know why. I'm not even sure when, but all of a sudden I found that I was crying. I mean, I hadn't fallen or anything. I hadn't even pinched a finger or banged my nose, yet here I was crying. I just curled up in a little ball and tucked my head in my arms and started to cry.

I'm not sure how long I sat there. I don't know how long I cried. I just know that finally I didn't seem to have any more tears.

I wiped my hand across my eyes to get rid of the last drops of moisture. My nose was running. I sniffed to get it under control.

I picked up my stick again but I didn't feel like

teasing the poor little ants any more. I sat and watched as they trekked back and forth, hauling load after load of something.

And then I felt an arm slip around me and draw me up close to a furry side.

"Barnaby," said a soft voice. "Barnaby, are you okay?"

It was Mother. I thought for sure that I would start to cry again but I managed not to. I tried to shake my head but it wouldn't work right.

She didn't say any more for a long time. She just held me tightly up against her like she used to do when I was very little. It felt—special.

"Are you worried?" she finally asked.

"Worried?" I managed with a sniff.

"About the new baby. Little Rosanna."

"I dunno," I said in a shaky voice.

"Do you think that she might take your place?" asked Mother.

"Well . . ."

"She won't, you know. No one will ever take your place."

Obviously, Mother hadn't been watching or listening to the humans at the big window.

"It's the sign," I said hotly. "No one changed it. No one made it say the right thing. Now they are all thinking that she is Number One, just like the sign says."

"Well . . ." said Mother slowly, and I could tell that she was trying to choose her words very carefully. "In a way, she is Number One."

My head came up. If Mother was trying to make

me feel better about things, she surely didn't have a very good way of doing it.

"She is the number one baby girl gorilla born most recently," said Mother, and then hurried on, "and you were the number one baby boy gorilla and the first baby gorilla to ever be born here at Roxbury Zoo. So you will always be Number One in that regard."

Her arm tightened about me.

"And you will always be Number One with me too," she went on. "Always."

"But . . . but . . . everyone treats Rosanna like . . . like . . . she was special," I blurted out, close to tears again.

"She is special," said Mother firmly.

I looked at Mother. She wasn't making much sense.

She lifted me up on her lap and cuddled me close.

"But I'm supposed to be the special one," I argued, resisting her hug.

"Oh, Barnaby," said Mother. "You are special. So very special. I love you so much."

She gave me another warm hug and rubbed her cheek against mine.

"Every baby born into our world is special. Very special. Don't you see? There isn't just one special person. The fact that little Rosanna is loved and cared for, doesn't make you any less special. There is always lots of love to go around. Lots of love. Love is like—like the air. You take a big breath of it and more just closes in around you. Love can never be exhausted. Or used up. For using love makes it grow bigger—and stronger—and more far-reaching."

"That little baby in there is just one more person to love you. One more person for you to love. She is special and you are special. Being in a family is special. It doesn't matter that the humans try to sort out who is number one. We are all number one—every one of us—in some way—to someone. If we weren't—if we couldn't be—then we wouldn't be here. There would be no reason for us to exist. But we are here. We are in a family and we are special to one another. That's what is important."

Mother's words and her warm, comforting arms were making me feel much better. I snuggled in against her.

"So, I'm still special?" I muttered. I just had to hear it said one more time. "I was the first one born here, so I'm special."

She hugged me close again and her eyes twinkled. "Yes, Barnaby. You are special. Not because you were born first. Not because you had your picture in the paper. Not because they put a big sign about you up on the wall. Not because all of the humans came to see this new baby in the zoo. No. That's not really why you're special. You are special because you are mine—and you are loved. I love you, Barnaby Gorilla. I love you."

And Mother gathered me close in her arms and rocked me gently back and forth.

I felt special. For the first time in my life, I think I really understood what it meant. I hoped with all of my heart that the new little baby, little Rosanna, would someday feel as special as I felt at that very moment.